EBURY PRESS

THE CANTONMENT CONSPIRACY

General Manoj Naravane (Retd) served as the twenty-eighth Chief of the Army Staff (COAS) of the Indian Army from 31 December 2019 to 30 April 2022. He is an alumnus of the National Defence Academy, Khadakwasla (Pune); the Indian Military Academy, Dehradun; the Defence Services Staff College, Wellington; and the Army War College, Mhow, where he was also on the faculty. In his distinguished military career spanning more than four decades, he also served as the Vice Chief of the Army Staff (VCOAS) and the General Officer Commanding-in-Chief (GOC-in-C) of the Training and Eastern Commands. He has vast experience in foreign affairs, having been part of the Indian Peace Keeping Force in Sri Lanka, a defence attaché at Yangon, Myanmar, and head of the Indian delegation to several countries. He also writes a bi-weekly column for The Print on matters of national security.

THE
CANTONMENT
CONSPIRACY

A MILITARY THRILLER

GENERAL
MANOJ NARAVANE

EBURY
PRESS

An imprint of Penguin Random House

EBURY PRESS

Ebury Press is an imprint of the Penguin Random House group of
companies whose addresses can be found at global.penguinrandomhouse.com

Published by Penguin Random House India Pvt. Ltd
4th Floor, Capital Tower 1, MG Road,
Gurugram 122 002, Haryana, India

First published in Ebury Press by Penguin Random House India 2025

ISBN 9780143471400

Typeset in Adobe Caslon Pro by MAP Systems, Bengaluru, India
Printed at Thomson Press India Private Limited

www.penguin.co.in

MIX
Paper | Supporting
responsible forestry
FSC® C010615

Contents

Prologue

Two shadows flitted through the moonlit night, but one of them was unaware of the other stalking it. The first shadow reached the boundary wall and went swiftly through a small gap that had been left to avoid cutting down a tree that used to be there. The gap now served as a discreet way to move to and from The Retreat, as the Officers' Mess was called, to the village of Muraguri beyond. The first shadow took a few moments to reorient itself, then moved towards a small *bagicha*, an orchard of mango trees that would allow it to reach the village unobserved.

The second shadow followed suit and was soon hot on the heels of the first, and both entered the orchard almost together. The villagers would later recount how horrified they had been to hear the blood-curdling sounds emanating from the orchard that had left them huddling in their huts. In the pale light of dawn, they had ventured out with *mashaals* in their hands, only to discover the mangled body of one of their women, a young, widowed girl of about twenty, almost stripped to the skin. What the girl was doing there was a mystery, but what was even more shocking than the look of terror on the girl's face were the long claw marks that stretched down the entire length of her semi-clothed back.

The police were called, but the clues were few. Ultimately it was declared an unnatural death and the blame put on a *tendua*, a leopard that had been sighted nearby a few days earlier. In fact, as a precautionary measure, a warning had been issued for the locals not to venture out during the hours of darkness and to keep their livestock indoors, for the tenduas were known to frequent the area, often making off with a chicken or even a pet dog or two. With their backs covered, the police and local administration were more than happy to wrap up the case. If they had looked closer, they may have perhaps noticed a nearly intact green rose, lying not far from the lifeless hand of the unfortunate girl. Badlu Prasad, the girl's father-in-law, was not convinced, but who listens to a poor villager? When questions were raised regarding Payal, his daughter-in-law's character, he soon fell silent. Life soon returned to normal, but the legend of the leopard only grew from year to year. And all that Badlu Prasad had to remind him of Payal was a solitary green rose.

Chapter 1

Onward Ho

Train number 14118, the Kalindi Express, chugged on to platform number 15 of the Old Delhi railway station. Lieutenant Rohit Verma, fresh out of the Indian Military Academy, watched impassively as the train shuddered to a halt amidst the melee of passengers clambering aboard. It was a strange feeling of déjà vu as almost two decades earlier, he had, as a child, caught the same train from Old Delhi to Farrukh Nagar, in western Uttar Pradesh. His father, Brigadier Madan Verma, formerly of the 17 Sikh Rifles, had just been posted as the Centre Commandant of the Sikh Rifles Regimental Centre at Fatehpuri, a short distance away from Farrukh Nagar, and the entire family was relocating there.

Rohit made his way to the first-class compartment, which was certainly an improvement on the earlier days.

He wondered if it was still a 'passenger' train for the early part of the journey when salespersons and *dudhwallahs* (milkmen) would barge into every bogie, reservation be damned, till they de-trained in clusters at various intermediate stations, not all of which were scheduled halts, as some of them would pull the emergency chain at will, forcing the train to halt. They had so perfected the art, knowing how long it took the train to slow down and come to a stop, that the train would halt right opposite their village, saving them the long trudge back. Due to this, the train was notorious for always being behind schedule. This would continue till around Tundla, which came at about 2 a.m., which was almost a third of the way to Farrukh Nagar, the scheduled arrival being 6.05 a.m. After Tundla, the train would pick up speed, the carriages rocking dangerously as the driver tried to make up for lost time. Until then, one had to bear with these unwanted companions, but it was still better than the alternative—having to face brigands who would target the train in the early hours of the morning as it passed through the notorious outlaw belt bordering the Chambal Valley. In fact, until the early 1980s, officers joining the Regimental Centre on commissioning were advised to travel in uniform as a measure of safety, should the train be looted. All officers travelled with a big black trunk, made to precise dimensions—100 cms long, 50 cms wide and 25 cms high—so that one could place a pair of trousers inside without having to fold it, a remnant of the era of starched clothes. The width and height calibrated so as to fit exactly under a first-class berth. However, even the dacoits knew that this imposing looking trunk, which all officers carried, had little of value, being full of army uniforms and accoutrements. Useful junk—as he used to tell his father.

Nevertheless, the danger was real. Only a few years earlier, Lieutenant AD Singh of the 11th Battalion, while travelling in the same area, had intervened when the moving train was being looted by armed dacoits. Grievously injured in trying to save his fellow passengers, he was posthumously awarded the Ashok Chakra, the highest peacetime award for gallantry. Fatehpuri was not for faint hearts. As he settled into his reserved berth, Rohit, a third-generation officer, wondered what the future had in store for him. His father and grandfather had both been in the army, in the same Regiment, and between them had fought in all of India's wars since Independence. Both were decorated soldiers, and it was partly their exploits and war stories that had motivated him to join the army. That and the countless years, his entire childhood in fact, spent moving from one army garrison to another, always in the company of the gallant jawans of the Regiment. He had been to half a dozen schools, in places whose names most people would have never even heard of and the entire country was his home. Rohit was the epitome of an army officer. Casually dressed, but well groomed even at this late hour, his demeanour exuded an assurance that stemmed from innate self-confidence. Nothing ever fazed him, not even snakes dropping in for dinner. Equally at home on the playing fields as in the classroom, his social etiquette had been honed by years of watching his father and mother; his mother especially, as she was the one who was around when his father was posted to far-off places, the names of which you were not even allowed to mention in the letters you wrote home. Even in that crowded compartment where everyone was jostling for space, one steely glance from him was enough to keep the unruly and unauthorized passengers at bay.

The train departed as scheduled on the dot of 10.50 p.m. (surprise, surprise!) only to lurch to a halt just as it was leaving the station. Rohit groaned inwardly. Nothing had changed in two decades after all; it was still a 'people's train' to board and deboard as per one's whims and fancies. This time though, the reason was different. As the passengers looked around, a uniformed person entered the compartment, a woman no less. Looking around in a determined manner and pushing the hulky dudhwallahs aside, she made her way to the 'A' cabin and greeted Rohit with an exclamation of joy and surprise. Rohit groaned a second time. Of all the luck, who should it be but his course-mate, Lieutenant Renuka Khatri, also commissioned at the same time. They were both from the 148th National Defence Academy (NDA) course, the first course that had admitted women into the NDA. Whereas Renuka had been in the Romeo Squadron earmarked exclusively for female cadets, Rohit had been in Juliet Squadron. As a result, Romeo and Juliet jokes abounded at the Academy. After three years at the NDA and another year at the IMA, as part of the 158th Regular course, they had both been commissioned into the army in June 2026. After two weeks of leave, they were now en route to the Centre for orientation training.

If Rohit was the epitome of an officer, Renuka was no less. In fact, in her uniform with the scarlet backings and shiny brass shoulder titles, the sight of her was enough to take one's breath away. The beret worn in exactly the correct regulation manner, the belt at her waist with its glinting buckle with the regimental crest, shiny black boots polished to perfection with not a smudge to show the travails of boarding the train. She sat down next to Rohit and took off her beret, her hair cascading down in a shimmering flow. She looked around in a defiant manner, as if challenging all the men around to say something, but all of them averted their gaze. No point taking *panga* (messing around) with this girl. The passengers made an interesting study of the nature of India. The smartly dressed officers, fragrant scents fighting to keep at bay the sturdy village folk returning after a hard day's work, redolent with the smell of sweat and stale milk.

As the train lurched off once again, the two of them looked at each other, wondering what twist of fate had brought them together. Sleeping was out of the question, what with all the unreserved passengers crowding the cabin. The least Rohit could do was offer Renuka the window seat beside him, as a flimsy shield from the rest of the burly crowd. By and by, the unreserved passengers got off, leaving them some breathing space, and to the rhythmic clacks of the train, both dozed off, each with their own apprehensions of the future.

Somewhere en route, in the early hours of the morning, just as the veil of darkness was lifting, Rohit sensed the presence of a leopard. The animal was moving stealthily towards him, even as Rohit stood transfixed, like a rabbit in the glare of headlights. One part of him told him he was on a train, there couldn't possibly be a leopard on board. Yet the feeling was so strong and when the leopard made a slash at him with long painted nails, Rohit uttered a cry and woke up in a pool of sweat, looking fearfully at Renuka, who was holding both his hands in a tight clasp.

There was no question of going back to sleep after that.

'You seem to have had a bad dream?' ventured Renuka.

'Yes,' replied Rohit with a shudder, 'a big leopard was chasing me, swiping at me with long painted claws. The strange thing is that I've had the same dream before, and the leopard keeps getting bigger and bigger.' He looked down as he spoke, and realized that they were still holding hands, which he hastily let go of with a start when he noticed that Renuka's nails were a bright shade of red.

Renuka was a little taken aback at this abrupt rejection but thought it better not to comment on it, though she did feel a little hurt. They talked a little more about where they had gone during their two-week break and what they had done. Renuka was from a small town just ahead of Shimla, where her father had an apple orchard. During the short break, she had wanted to help out at the farm, pruning the apple trees and doing other sundry jobs, but her father would have none of it. 'You are an officer now,' he said. 'While there's no harm in getting your hands dirty once in a while, you have to now be more of a manager.' She had no army background, though a distant *chacha* (uncle) had been in the army. She had hardly ever met him but his demeanour and the action-packed photos in his prized album, hinting of a life of adventure in exotic places, had been the inspiration to join the army. During her school days, she had also joined the National Cadet Corps (NCC), even participating in the Republic Day parade as part of the NCC contingent. Not only was Renuka from the first batch of female cadets admitted to the NDA/IMA but she was only one of the first two women officers to have been commissioned into a fighting arm—the Infantry. This, in itself, was a momentous decision taken by the army headquarters, as till now, women officers were only commissioned into the supporting arms and services. As one of the first women officers in the Infantry, that too in a regiment with a chequered past, Renuka would have a lot to prove. She would not only have to be good at her job but do it better than her male counterparts. The weight of expectations lay heavy on her shoulders, keeping her always supercharged, not allowing herself to lower her guard, ever.

Rohit, on the other hand, was a third-generation army officer. It was based on this affiliation—parental claim—

that Rohit had been commissioned in the same unit and Regiment as his father and grandfather, 17 Sikh Rifles. He had grown up in army bases and cantonments and had been the pesky kid wandering around the unit lines, coming in everyone's way. He knew most of the officers and their wives, and in a manner of speaking, even the men. They had bounced him on their shoulders as a kid, taught him all the games—football, hockey and basketball—which had stood him in good stead at the Academy. He had also picked up their colourful vocabulary, which had equally stood him in good stead when he became a cadet appointment and had to dress-down unruly juniors. As compared to Renuka, he had an easier transition to look forward to, but the weight of expectations lay equally heavily on his shoulders, even if for the exact opposite reasons, with both having to prove that they were worthy.

Rohit glanced at Renuka as these thoughts surfaced, wondering how she would fare. Should he try to take her under his wing or let her fend for herself? No, he thought to himself, the Academy had groomed them all to be fearless, independent leaders; it would not do to break that trust. Let her learn the ropes in her own way. He would have her back as a course-mate, nothing more. Farrukh Nagar was nearing, and he nudged her awake so that they could both freshen up before alighting at the railway station. Most of the passengers had detrained somewhere en route, so they had the coupé to themselves. They made an odd pair. Renuka looked quite officer-like, albeit in a slightly crumpled uniform with the distinctive scarlet shoulder titles and the two shiny stars of a full Lieutenant, beret at the regulation angle. In comparison, Rohit, in faded jeans and T-shirt, tatty golf cap worn backwards, sneakers that had seen better days and with a day-old stubble, looked like a kid going home for the summer break. Chalk and cheese.

Even as the train rolled to a halt, Renuka and Rohit started unloading their luggage, manoeuvring their odd-shaped trunks and suitcases. Earlier, the train used to terminate at Farrukh Nagar, and they could unload their luggage at leisure. Now, however, the train went on up to Kanpur, and there was only a five-minute halt, so they had to help each other get their luggage out into the vestibule. Alighting on the platform, they were met by the reception party, Havildar Pritam Singh and two more jawans, one of whom was bearing a tray of steaming hot tea and pakoras. That was one thing that one could be assured of. No matter the time of the day or the place, airport or railway station, tea and pakoras would always be forthcoming. Taking a steaming tumbler of tea and biting into a crunchy pakora,

Rohit sighed in satisfaction, giving Pritam a big *jappi* (hug), as it was none other than Pritam who had seen him off when he had left to join the Academy four years earlier, when the unit had been at Meerut. Seeing Pritam was like a homecoming and lessened his earlier apprehensions.

'*Twade nall ik aur nave Leftenant sahib ane sigge?* [Another new Lieutenant was to come with you],' inquired Pritam, looking around but not registering Lieutenant Renuka Khatri standing right before him in full uniform. Rohit gave him a nudge in the ribs, and it was a sight to behold when Pritam finally registered who the other new, young officer was. Women officers had been in the army for decades, some were even commanding battalions, but a woman officer in the Sikh Rifles? Unthinkable, or as his *Tau* used to say, '*dimak chakarch pe gaya* [I just cannot fathom it].' However, training took over and snapping off a smart salute, Pritam extended all courtesies due to an officer. After checking that all the luggage was accounted for, they made their way to the parking lot, where the transport to take them to Fatehpuri was parked. Although it was still early morning, the flies buzzing around, the languid pace of the coolies, the general air of laissez-faire, made it seem as if time had stood still, these last fifteen years. The hustle and excitement of a metro was lacking. If ever there were to be an example of a mofussil town, this was it. Stopping in front of the vehicle, Pritam looked at them thoughtfully. Seeing the two of them, both officers of equal seniority, had plunged Pritam into a dilemma.

For a couple of freshly minted Lieutenants and other personnel who might have been on the same train, the Centre had sent a 2.5-ton truck, *dhai ton* as they were affectionately called, large enough to carry all the luggage but not really catering for passengers. As per the rules, apart from the driver, the next senior-most person occupied the front or co-driver's seat, while all the others sat in the body or bed of the truck on hard slatted benches, most preferring to stand, with their heads poking out. Pritam was in a fix, who should occupy the front seat? The uniformed woman officer or Rohit in his faded jeans? Technically, both were of equal seniority, so what should he do? The first priority should go to the uniformed person, but Rohit was his protégé. He couldn't possibly offend either. If the unit personnel came to know that he made Rohit sit in the back of the truck in favour of some female, he would never hear the last of it. They could both squeeze in on the front seat; it was big enough for two skinny young officers, but that would be an infringement of the rules. Rohit could sense his trepidation; after all, he had spent his childhood days with army personnel. Such apparent seniority issues were not new to him.

'Pritam,' he said, 'after all these years, I'm not quite sure about the route to the Centre. Why don't you sit in front and guide us? We will both get into the back and be with the rest of the boys.' Pritam smiled, snapping off a smart salute of relief. Renuka and Rohit clambered into the back of the 'dhai ton,' Renuka ignoring Rohit's helping hand, and they set off on the short forty-five-minute ride to Fatehpuri.

Chapter 2

SRRC

The dhai-ton rattled through the streets of Farrukh Nagar towards Fatehpuri, the home of the Sikh Rifles Regimental Centre or SRRC. It was still early morning, and the city was just coming to life. Good thing too, as later in the day, the traffic in the lanes and by-lanes would be a nightmare with all kinds of transportation, from swanky cars and motorcycles, trucks and tractor-trolleys to pedal-rickshaws and pushcarts, all vying for space. Bullock carts and herds of cattle were not uncommon sights, and if one were to get stuck behind one of these, then getting off and walking would probably be a faster way of reaching one's destination.

The truck was full of men, some returning from leave, some going to the Centre for their discharge drill, the final formalities before proceeding on pension, as well as new recruits, the Agniveers, going to the Centre for the first time for their basic training. Rohit soon struck up a conversation with many of them. One of the non-commissioned officers (NCOs), Gurnam, was from the same unit and they exchanged tales of when Gurnam would sneak extra *karha* prasad from the gurudwara for Rohit and his younger sister, Aradhana. With the recruits he joked that we are in the same boat—fresh blood for the army. Renuka sat silent throughout the journey, observing the easy manner in which Rohit fitted in, and wondered whether she would ever be in the same standing, with the spontaneous and easy acceptance that Rohit got. Her early attempts to strike up a conversation had failed, the men intimated as much by the uniform as by the fact that she was a woman. Renuka realized that these were twin barriers that she would have to overcome, her gender as well as her lack of background.

They soon entered Fatehpuri, turning right opposite the War Memorial and towards the Officers' Mess and single officers' quarters. While their luggage was being unloaded, Havildar Pritam informed them that they were expected in the adjutant's office in the main administrative block by 0900 hours. It was almost 0800 hours by then, barely enough time to get organized. Rohit whizzed into his room, unpacked his uniform which he had kept uppermost in his trunk and gave it to the room bearer for ironing. By the time he showered and shaved, his uniform was neatly laid out on the bed. By 0845 hours he was ready and rearing to go, fresh as a daisy. The transport had left, so they had to walk up to the administrative block about a kilometre away and were there five minutes before the appointed time.

The adjutant, Major Vikrant Kale, welcomed them warmly, though he did glance a little disapprovingly at Renuka's crumpled uniform and slightly dishevelled appearance. A little shy of six feet with steely grey eyes and a close-cropped moustache, it was his responsibility to maintain discipline and keep the Centre ticking. A mere rumour that he was on his rounds would give everyone the jitters. Bidding them to sit down at an adjoining table, he gave them a set of forms to fill out, including the all-important one for the Controller of Defence Accounts (Officers)—CDA (O), Pune—which was the payment disbursing authority for all officers of the army. Then, after a quick cup of tea and samosas, it was time for the commandant's interview. As they walked in and saluted, Rohit felt quite at ease. He had been to this very office many times before when his father had been the commandant. The wood-panelled office adorned with the regimental flag and other trophies and artefacts was awe-inspiring.

He instinctively looked at the appointment board behind the ornate office table, searching for his father's name. Yes, there it was, Brigadier Madan Verma, from May 2010 to August 2012 and already there were half a dozen names after that. The commandant was a kindly-looking man with greying hair and moustache, with a twinkle in his eyes that hinted at a mischievous past. Lost in his reverie and not paying attention, Rohit realized that the commandant, Brigadier Ashok Menon, was giving him a stern look.

'Rohit,' he said, 'don't expect me to cut you any slack just because your father was the commandant. As far as I am concerned, you and Renuka here are on an equal footing.' Renuka stood silently at attention, not daring to look left or right. At ease, he had told her, continuing by welcoming them all and saying how happy he was to see such a fine lot of officers join the Regiment. He reminded them that the Regiment was now their family and the honour of the Regiment sacrosanct.

'Yes, Sir,' Rohit replied but his eyes were still wandering around the office, as he was overcome by a wave of nostalgia. The commandant was not amused by his inattentiveness. 'Rohit!' he called out again, more sternly this time. 'Behave yourself. I am not impressed by your attitude; this is not your pop's joint to do as you please. Remember you are on probation—one small misstep, and I'll have your Commission annulled.' With that warning, he asked the adjutant to march them out and then come back. 'Keep an eye out for that blighter Rohit,' advised the commandant. 'Just because he's third generation and his father a former commandant, he is getting wrong ideas that his lineage will carry him through. Keep an eye on Renuka, too,' he added paternally. 'She has a tough time ahead trying to match up. Being the first woman officer in the Infantry is also going to be weighing on her.'

'Yes, Sir!'

'We will be fair but no favours or concessions—men or women, or background,' he concluded, turning back to the papers on his desk.

A familiarization tour of the Centre followed. Apart from the Sikh Rifles, Fatehpuri was also the home of the Frontier Force Regimental Centre (FFRC), and several of their batchmates had been commissioned in various battalions of the Frontier Force Regiment. During their round as well as on subsequent days, they would often bump into each other and exchange notes. The FFRC had been in Fatehpuri much longer and was more well established. The SRRC had moved to Fatehpuri only after the 1971 Indo-Pak War that led to the liberation of East Pakistan and the creation of Bangladesh. At one end of the cantonment was a small fort, which had in the nineteenth century been garrisoned by a detachment of the Sikh Pioneers, the forebears of the Sikh Rifles. There was therefore a tenuous link to the SRRC being located there.

Much had changed in the intervening years. Although the general layout remained the same, everything looked so much more modern. They went round the recruit training companies, each named after a battle honour earned by the Regiment in the various wars it had fought, Poonch, Parbat Ali, Kalidhar and Bogra. Then to the various training areas, ranges and finally to the drill square. Training was on in full swing and the hoarse cries from the drill-square mingled with the crack of rifle fire at the short ranges. In his excitement, Rohit kept pointing out various landmarks and explaining how they had been earlier. His remarks were received with interest, but as time wore on, his batchmates became quite exasperated by his constant interruptions. They were also taken to the regimental gurudwara, where they paid obeisance to the Guru Granth Sahib, and were each presented with a traditional Sikh *kada*, a religious symbol that represents the eternal nature of God and serves as a reminder to live righteous and faithful lives. The tour also included a quick stop at the Officers' Mess. While leaving the Mess, Renuka remarked, 'Look at those two *malis*. What shammers they are. They haven't moved an inch since we got here.' Rohit laughed out loud, 'Look more closely, my dear friends. They are statues only, but so lifelike that almost everyone is fooled by them.'

Altogether, eight of them had been commissioned into the Regiment, and they were distributed two officers to each of the training companies, as understudies to the respective company commanders. Since they had arrived together, Rohit and Renuka found themselves together yet again as part of Kalidhar Training Company. The company commander, Lieutenant Colonel Moti Singh, with about nineteen years of service, was of the old school and thoroughly disapproved of women being in the army, let alone the infantry. Slightly bitter at having been overlooked for promotion, due to an operational lapse many years ago that had blighted his career, his moustache danced mesmerizingly whenever he spoke, which was often, since he had an opinion on everything under the sun. He was also usually the butt of jokes arising from his name; either Moti Mahal after a famous restaurant chain, but more often, as '*Mota*' Singh Sahib, 'fatso,' a term especially favoured by the jawans on account of his large girth.

'What a silly idea,' he said when Rohit and Renuka reported to the company. 'Women in the combat arms!' Least concerned that Renuka was standing right in front of him, he turned to his Junior Commissioned Officer (JCO) platoon commander, Subedar Dilbagh Singh, and muttered in chaste Punjabi, '*Sadde jawan mundyanun nahin chhadte, te is kudi da ki hovega*? [Our soldiers don't even spare young boys—what will happen to this girl?]' Dilbagh gave a full-throated laugh which was too much for Rohit to bear. 'You can't say such things,' he admonished the company commander. 'If we as officers stoop to such levels, how can we expect the men to rise up to ours?' This in turn was too much for Moti Singh to accept.

'Shut up, you pipsqueak,' he thundered, the tips of his moustache quivering dangerously. 'Don't think that just because your father was in the army you can say whatever you want and get away with it. *Bade dekhen hain tere jaise lallu* [I've seen a lot of morons like you].' Rohit was about to launch himself at his superior when he was restrained by a gentle hand on his shoulder.

'It's all right, Rohit,' said Renuka. 'We have heard worse when we were at the Academy. The sooner we develop a thick skin, the better. If we let these emotions rule us, we will never be able to function.' Although tempers were running high, the moment passed, and they went on with their work.

In the evening though, when they had all gathered in the Officers' Mess for dinner, Rohit broached the subject again. 'What did you mean when you said in the morning that you've been treated much worse?'

All of them were there—Naresh, well-built and a product of the Punjab Public School, Nabha; Chaudhari, lanky and bespectacled with tousled hair; and Govardhan, from Sainik School, Amravathi, who could barely speak Hindi, let alone Punjabi. Listening to Govardhan giving out instructions in Hindi during their Academy days had been some of the 'humour in uniform' moments. 'Let it be,' said Renuka, but when pressed, she launched into a monologue, all her suppressed emotions coming to the fore.

'You guys had it easy, we had to fight tooth and nail for everything. Superficially, we were feted as the first girl cadets to join the Academy, but there was always an undercurrent of resentment.' Rohit was reminded of the morning's exchange with the company commander and had to agree that there seemed to be a kernel of truth in what she was saying. 'It's not anyone's fault,' she continued. 'The Academy was a male preserve for so long that some things just didn't seem to strike the authorities.'

'Like what?' chorused the officers.

'Take double outdoors, for instance,' she elaborated. 'It's fine for all of you to be changing in the open, but we couldn't possibly do that. Some cabins were made for us, but obviously not 100 per cent, so some of us would invariably be late for the next parade. Nobody understood our problems and just thought that we were shammers who didn't have it in us to make the grade or that we were using our gender as a shield.'

The young men were silent for a while as they re-imagined the most dreaded of programmes, PT followed by drill, where one had to carry a full set of uniform draped over the handlebars of the cycle, drill-shoes hanging ponderously on either side. After PT, they would all rush to the cycle stand outside the Drill Square, undress and dress in drill order within the ten minutes between two periods. There was no modesty involved—but they had never really thought about how the girl cadets managed to do this Houdini-type dress-changing act.

'Well, that's all in the past,' said Naresh, another of the course-mates. 'We are all officers now, and look on the bright side: while we are all doubling up, you have a room to yourself.'

'That's exactly the attitude I am talking about,' retorted Renuka. 'You'll always think you are doing us women officers some kind of favour or granting a special privilege. Unless you get these kinds of prejudices out of your head, we will never be treated as equals. Just think of what Mota Singh said this morning,' she added bitterly, using the company commander's nickname, 'he is not fit to be an officer.'

The other officers looked at Rohit inquisitively, but before he could answer, who should walk in but Lieutenant Colonel Moti Singh himself. 'Ah so,' he said, apparently having heard the last part of their conversation. 'Who is not fit to be an officer?'

All of them got quite flustered and tongue-tied on seeing the senior officer and it fell upon Rohit to retrieve the situation.

'Nothing, Sir, we were just talking about one of our course-mates.' Signalling discreetly to the steward who had just entered the anteroom, he asked Moti Singh, 'What would you like to drink, Sir?'

'Get me a large rum,' Moti Singh told the steward. 'And get some snacks too—masala peanuts will be fine.' Settling his large bulk on to one of the sofas, he proceeded to tell the 'youngsters' all about the Regiment and the highlights of his brilliant career, right from his commissioning days. Coming ultimately to the recent past, he made it sound as if he had single-handedly battled the Chinese during the skirmishes in Eastern Ladakh. The rum kept flowing, the stories unending, and they tried hard to suppress their yawns, rolling their eyes at some particularly preposterous anecdote. 'But what to do,' he said finally, glaring at Rohit, 'one cannot fight fate. My CO was against me—did not even recommend me for any gallantry award. And now I am stuck in this shitty place chaperoning shitheads like you.' With that, he lumbered to his feet and went towards the exit. The officers got up hastily to their feet and chorused, 'Goodnight, Sir.' That seemed to trigger another thought because he stopped abruptly at the door and turning around, said in a casually sinister manner, 'BPET[1] tomorrow morning at 0500 hours.' Seeing their stunned looks he tossed off the last bumper for the night. 'Don't drink too much!' as if it was them and not him, who had been doing all the drinking.

*　*　*

The young officers were kept busy with various training activities, including learning all about the Regiment, its history and ethos. The outdoor training activities were carried out in the cooler morning hours. They would all go to the rifle ranges, where they not only honed their skills but also learnt how the soldiers were trained, something

---

[1] Battle Physical Efficiency Tests

that they would have to do themselves once they joined their respective units. A lot of their time was spent on the drill square but with a difference. This time around they were not the ones under training but had to train the new recruits, which was easier said than done. Most came from village backgrounds and were overawed by their surroundings. It was only the experience and patience of the NCOs that kept them focused, both of which the young officers were lacking. When it was their turn to drill a squad, the words of command were all messed up, resulting in the squads getting all jumbled up and even colliding with each other. The NCOs had a jolly good laugh at their expense, reporting back to the training in-charge '*nave leftnent sahib sare gwachi gan hainge* [the new lieutenants are all hopelessly inept/lost cases].'

Renuka was at the forefront of all activities, so much so that she earned the sobriquet of '*keen kumari*' or eager beaver. Keen kumars/kumaris were frowned upon as their enthusiasm often resulted in extra work for the rest of the group. In the morning PT when a slow jog would have sufficed, Renuka would surge ahead, leaving the others no choice but to pick up speed. In the field and battle craft class, she would crawl from one bush to another as if there was actual enemy fire raining down on them. They had to crawl too, otherwise their instructor would shout derisively, 'See, even this chit of a girl is better than all of you.'

'C'mon *yaar*,' remonstrated Rohit, 'just take it easy. We are not at the Academy any more, being assessed for every activity. Relax, and have fun. Once we join our units, we will be busy as hell.'

Renuka heard him out before replying with a touch of sarcasm, 'Typical third-generation officer response. You think you can just coast along, doing the bare minimum work, just because your father and grandfather were in the army. I have no such *chhatra chhaya* (godfather) to protect me.'

Rohit was hurt by this unjust allegation, and he turned away disappointed that she should think so. Yes, he had the benefit of pedigree, but it was not his father who had come first in the cross-country run or been awarded the best firer trophy. It was his sweat and hard work that had earned him those accolades. Rohit shrugged philosophically—parental claim rubs both ways he reasoned, one has to take the good with the bad—and there would always be a few jealous people around. His father had been a strict disciplinarian, and there was always the possibility of someone who felt wronged getting back at his father by targeting him.

* * *

A few days into their stay, the commandant invited them to his residence, Khanda House, for cocktails. Rohit was no stranger to the house, having stayed there as a child. The commandant's residence was a stately colonial house overlooking the River Ganga. To the front of the house were a series of stepped lawns, descending towards the river. During the monsoons, when the river was in spate, its waters came right up the bottom-most step. On this step was a large brooding pipal tree, the focal point around which many a ghost story was spun. In hindsight, thought Rohit, his mother must have spun those yarns to keep them from going too close to the water, as the river was known for its dangerous whirlpools that could sweep away even a strong swimmer in its currents.

The house itself was quite quaint, with several rooms and passageways that had recessed or hidden alcoves, ideal for playing hide-and-seek. Once seated in the drawing room, Rohit looked around to see what had changed. The basic layout seemed the same, though there was a doorway he could not recollect, and he wondered where possibly it led to. After drinks were served, Mrs Menon came in and offered some mouth-watering galouti kebabs, which literally melted in one's mouth. 'These are excellent,' complimented Rohit, adding, 'they remind me of what our cook Zareena used to make when Dad was posted here.'

Mrs Menon was taken aback and said, '*Arre*, our cook is also Zareena, could she possibly be the same person? I do know she has been around for a long time. Let me call her and check.'

Zareena was called for and despite the passage of time, Rohit recognized her straightaway. She had not only been their cook but also his minder of sorts as he used to be a naughty young lad and used to roam around all over the grounds with her daughter Rehmat, who she would often get along.

Zareena had tears in her eyes, 'How tall my *baba* has become! An officer like his father.' Rohit wanted to give her a hug, but it was a formal setting in the commandant's house, so he thought better of it. He waved to her from across the room, signalling with his hands that he would meet her later.

On the way back to their rooms, Rohit couldn't stop talking about his erstwhile nanny and her daughter Rehmat. 'We used to go everywhere together,' he said. 'Exploring the house and the gardens, sometimes sneaking into the Officers' Mess. On the other side was big house belonging to a rich businessman, who was quite a *khadoos* character, always grumpy and boorish, who used to shoo us away. Reminded me rather of Mr Wilson, and we were like older versions of Dennis and Gina.'

'Oh! So now we know who your childhood sweetheart was,' joked Renuka, making all the others laugh out loud, finally putting an end to Rohit's ramblings.

Walking towards the Officers' Mess the next morning, Rohit noticed a few civilians around a *mazhar*, a shrine to a mystic of yesteryears, that lay about midway to the Mess. It was a Thursday, and he remembered that on Thursdays, a lot of people came there throughout the day to offer prayers and seek some boon or the other. It was said that it was the shrine of a famous saint from the eighteenth century, and while Rohit didn't believe much in such things, he was not one to question others' faiths and beliefs. It used to be a small grave covered with a green cloth at the base of a mango tree, but it had grown in proportion and now had a gate and railing enclosing the shrine with a tiled platform all around for worshipers to circumambulate.

As he was walking past, he heard a soft voice calling his name from behind a thick hedge, 'Rohit, Rohit!' He paused, looked closer and noticed a young girl standing there, dressed in an attractive light blue salwar-kurta, hair tied neatly behind in a pigtail. 'Rohit—it's me, Rehmat.

Ammi told me she saw you yesterday at the commandant's house,' said the girl.

Rohit was pleasantly surprised. He had indeed been thinking about her the whole night and how to find out more about her whereabouts. 'Rehmat, how great to see you,' he said, moving towards her through a gap in the hedge. Rohit had grown into a handsome young officer, but Rehmat had surpassed him, becoming an exquisitely beautiful damsel.

'Fate has brought us together again,' and so saying, he impulsively gave her a big hug as childhood friends would. 'I have to rush to work,' he told her, 'but we must meet again. This is my mobile number; give me a call so that we can plan something.' Sensing some hesitation, he added, 'If not, I'll wait for you by the rose garden in the Officers' Mess.'

Rehmat nodded silently, overcome by emotion. She gave him a quick peck on his cheek, before running off towards the woods leading to her home in the nearby village, hiding her face in her hands, pigtail bouncing joyously and alluringly from side to side.

Rohit was in a trance for the rest of the day. At the firing ranges, he had a washout—a zero score—having fired mistakenly at the wrong target. At drill practice, he forgot to give the command of 'Column halt!,' with the result that his squad kept marching till it reached the end of the drill square. His absent-mindedness was evident.

'Is everything all right?' asked Renuka, touching him solicitously on the shoulder. 'I hope you're feeling well, you hardly touched your breakfast.' He brushed her hand away and now it was her turn to be hurt. What a strange character he is, she thought. Sometimes he jumps to my defence, and at other times, he ignores me to the point of indifference. For Rohit though, nothing mattered. All he could see was an ethereal beauty in blue, with a swaying pigtail, his face still tingling from where her lips had brushed his cheek.

That evening, after the games parade, Rohit rushed back and changing quickly into civvies, left the room, making some feeble excuse to his roommate. 'I've got to get some stuff from the market. See you later in the Mess.' Knowing that all eyes were on him, he purposely turned towards the market, which was on the opposite side of the Mess. Once out of sight, he took a small service lane which he remembered from his childhood days, which exited near the Mess. Entering the Mess, he went swiftly towards the rose garden and scouted around for any signs of Rehmat. I hope she comes, he thought, hoping that she had not taken his impromptu hug amiss. On the other hand, she had given him a fleeting kiss, so that must be a good sign.

Just as he was giving up hope, he saw some movement in the gathering dusk. He had been looking towards the main gate, little realizing that Rehmat couldn't possibly come through there with the sentry at the entrance. He recalled now that small gap in the boundary wall, left there for some unknown reason, through which Rehmat slipped through effortlessly. Seeing Rohit, she rushed towards him, and they were soon in a tight embrace. Amidst the heady fragrance of the rose garden and fireflies twinkling in the dark, they exchanged their first kiss. Lost in their world, they did not notice amidst the twinkling fireflies, a mysterious pair of eyes watching them from the shadows.

Chapter 3

Dining-In Shemozzle

As part of tradition, all officers on Commissioning are formally welcomed into the Regiment, or dined in, to the Regiment. For the newly commissioned officers, it was a great moment to receive a personalized invitation, requesting the pleasure of their company to dinner at the Officers' Mess the coming Saturday. The invitation was on a crisp ivory card, with the Khanda, the regimental insignia embossed in the Regiment's distinctive scarlet. The language was as per what they had learnt at the Academy, and practised writing in their service writing classes. Down to the RSVP in the bottom left corner and the dress to be worn—(6B)—in the bottom right corner.

The Officers' Mess is one of the most hallowed institutions of any establishment. It is not only a home away from home but a source of pride where the honour and glory of the Regiment is on display. The Sikh Rifles Regimental Centre Officers' Mess, affectionately named 'The Retreat,' was no different. The Mess was run by a Mess committee, but the real force was Head Butler Jeevan Singh, who kept it running like clockwork. The first day, they had been welcomed to the Mess by Jeevan, who took it upon himself to explain the history of the Mess to the young officers. Jeevan had been in the army himself, and after his retirement, had been employed in a civilian capacity to manage the Mess.

The building originally belonged to a British officer when British troops had been garrisoned at Fatehpuri. The officer had run up a large number of debts to clear which, he had sold the property to a local businessman, who had bought it as a place for his ailing wife, hence 'The Retreat'. At the time of Independence, his wife having passed away, he donated the property to the Indian Army in a display of patriotism. His only request being that the name should not be changed, which was honoured.

The inside of the building was a veritable museum. Solid leather sofa sets and polished teak furniture made up the seating area. Carpets from far corners of the world adorned the floors. Silver trophies, each commemorating some major event or victory in battle, were placed strategically around the anteroom. One of the more interesting pieces was an ornate brass seal belonging to the Dalai Lama, which had been brought back by the Younghusband Expedition of 1904, which sought to establish British influence in Tibet and counter Russian influence in the region, as well as to solve the boundary dispute between Tibet and Sikkim. The boundary dispute got further complicated when the Chinese forcibly occupied Tibet and the unresolved boundary was the reason for Sino-Indian War of 1962 as well as the frequent clashes between the two armies, the latest being the clash in Eastern Ladakh in 2020. Seeing and hearing all this made a chill run down their spines; they were part of this history from now onwards. The walls were mounted with hunting trophies and delicate porcelain plates. The dining room was equally splendid with a 'U'-shaped table which could easily seat fifty people for a formal sit-down dinner. For everyday dining, there was less formal seating, in a separate room closer to the kitchens, attached to which was also a ladies' room. Leading off from the anteroom was an arched doorway to the bar, its mirrored backdrop reflecting a wide array of wines and spirits.

The pièce de résistance, however, was the mounting in the arched doorway of a large leopard, eyes glinting, mouth open in a snarl, one paw raised to strike, as if guarding the entrance to the bar, its expression echoing the quote on the arch, 'Abandon all hope, ye who enter here'.

'This leopard mounting is more than a hundred years old, shot by the British officer who owned the building,' said Jeevan. 'It's a female and her progeny are said to roam even today.'

'Does it have a name?' asked Renuka.

'Some of the village folks used to call her "Bijli" because she was as fast as lightning, but now we just call her "Tendu". It seems more affectionate,' replied Jeevan.

As they moved ahead, Renuka nudged Rohit in the ribs, 'I hope this is not the girl of your dream, your *sapnon ki rani.*'

The tour of the Mess continued on other days, with Jeevan as their guide. The artefacts were too numerous to describe—from a gold-plated tea set, to a stuffed python slithering on the wall, which sent shivers down their spines. A tiger's paw in a glass case, shared the wall with Mughal miniature paintings, some quite erotic in nature. Each wall was packed with numerous artefacts, with no semblance of order. It could do with some curating, thought Renuka but kept her opinion to herself. Jeevan knew the history of each piece, down to the number of books in the library. 'Do make note of these facts,' he cautioned, 'there might be a question or two on the Mess during your dining-in.'

On the appointed day, they all changed into their 6Bs—white half-sleeved shirt and black trousers with the cummerbund in red, blue and old gold, and scarlet-coloured side cap. Fresh out of the Academy, they were slim and trim, good-looking young people. Renuka looked particularly alluring, the tight cummerbund highlighting her figure, and Naresh almost mouthed a 'wow' before stopping himself. Does one say 'wow' to one's course-mates? Throughout the week, as trainee officers, they had been going on foot all over the Centre from the Mess to the training areas and back. Today though, since they were guests, two SUVs had been detailed to ferry them to the Mess.

'Behave yourselves, lads,' cautioned Rohit, who had seen many a dining-in. 'Everyone will try to ply us with drinks, to see whether we make fools of ourselves or overstep social norms. So let's keep an eye out for each other.'

'Who will be there?'

'The commandant and his wife Priya, of course. Plus, all the officers and their lady wives and perhaps their grown-up children. I have known the Bahadurs from before and they have two charming daughters, who are sure to be around. There will be singing and dancing and even a few party games, where we will be paired with some lady or the other. The kids will be looking up to us as role models, so best behaviour—remember, even a party is like being on parade, on duty, so to say.'

Excited by the thoughts of dancing and party games but considerably sobered up by Rohit's advice, they clambered into the waiting cars and sped off to the Mess. They had been going to the Mess throughout the week, but this time it looked totally different. The driveway right from the entrance gate to the lawns had fairy lights on the hedges and decorative bushes. Drop lights twinkled in the branches of the bigger trees. The Mess building had been lit up and it conjured images of a distant romantic past. The regimental band in full regalia were in the bandstand. The lawn was dotted with a few tall round tables and there was scattered seating spread all over. There were no dinner tables or chairs, as dinner would be a formal affair in the main dining room served with bone-china crockery and silver cutlery, taken out only on very special occasions. As guests, they arrived last, and the sounds of music and laughter were drifting across the lawns.

'Welcome to the Regiment,' said the commandant, shaking each one by the hand, the official photographer bustling around clicking everyone from all angles.

'Good evening, Sir. Good evening, Mrs Menon,' they replied, a bit uncertainly, not used to being the centre of attention. On seeing them come in, the officers and ladies formed a loose semicircle, and they went around and introduced themselves. They had all met the officers during their training and familiarization rounds, but this was the first time that they were meeting them and their wives socially. Some of the couples looked made for each other, but others were quite a contrast. 'Mota' Singh's wife Manpreet was a dainty little lady with dimpled cheeks and a tinkling laugh.

'Hello, Rohit,' she said, 'my husband has been telling me a lot of stories about you.'

'Good things I hope, ma'am,' said Rohit, wondering what good things, considering they had been at loggerheads ever since that fractious exchange the very first day. Rohit met the Bahadurs and their daughters Roma and Shoma, who had grown up to become beautiful young ladies. 'Hello Rona–Dhona,' said Rohit teasingly, and they pouted back at him, though secretly pleased that he had remembered their nicknames.

'Good evening, uncle,' they replied sweetly, in a tone reserved for an elderly person.

'What bloody uncle,' spluttered Rohit, and they had a hearty laugh at his discomfiture. The other officers crowded around, eager to be introduced to the young ladies and were soon immersed in small talk, the girls giggling uproariously at every silly joke.

'Hello, Renuka,' said Manpreet Kaur, clasping her by the hand and pulling her towards the other ladies, 'you have to absolutely tell us all about your experiences as a woman in uniform.' Renuka looked helplessly back at Rohit. She would rather be with her course-mates and the other officers with whom she had more in common. Rohit gave her a wry smile and with a wave of his hand, whispered in her ear that he would rescue her soon. Renuka laughed at the thought of getting rescued from the ladies, but it cheered her, nonetheless. This brief exchange was not lost on the all-seeing eyes of the ladies, who were thrilled at the prospect of a budding romance. Some more juicy gossip.

Rohit excused himself from the others and went to talk with the commandant, who was surrounded by other officers, discussing regimental matters. 'Come Rohit,' said the commandant seeing him approach, 'do join us.'

Rohit clinked glasses and merged into the group, listening attentively to their views on different subjects, from international relations to current affairs and sports. The officers were well read and gave fresh perspectives to what he had read in the papers, specially the military aspects of important events.

'What do you think of the situation in Bangladesh?' asked the commandant and it took a while for Rohit to realize that the question was addressed to him.

'It is almost two years since the student protests, and the overthrow of the Sheikh Hasina government. There is a semblance of normality. But unless the basic issues are tackled, such as poverty and unemployment, simmering tensions will remain and the situation can blow up again.'

'That's a good point,' said the commandant, turning to the others. 'And we must keep that in mind for ourselves too. If there is too much social inequality, it is bad for any country.'

The band was playing some evergreen numbers, alternating between Bollywood songs and English classics. '*Gore Gore O Banke Chhore*' from the 1950s movie *Samadhi* was one such tune. His father had heard it as a child and later as an officer, as he too was hearing it now. Seventy-five years or so later, it was still going strong. No Mess party was complete without this song playing at least once, and more often than not, it was the signal to commence dancing. This evening was no different and soon a few couples made their way to the dance floor. Rohit was familiar with the pattern. There would be few slow, nostalgic numbers to begin with, to get everyone in the mood. Then the tempo would pick up, by which time a couple of drinks would have gone down the hatch, and then the dancing would begin in earnest, stately foxtrots and waltzes, giving way to more popular Bollywood dance tunes. Being in a Sikh Rifles Regiment, the traditional *bhangra* would make its entry sometime or the other, in which everyone would have to join in, like it or not.

Looking around the lawns, Rohit saw that Renuka was momentarily alone, and went to rescue her as promised. 'Oh, taking her for a dance,' trilled one of the ladies with a knowing smile. Rohit had not really thought about that but now he had no choice but to ask Renuka for a dance. Rohit and Renuka felt as if all eyes were on them as they made their way to the dance floor. Their course-mates, thrilled at this turn of events, gave them much encouragement, and added their two bits to the already charged atmosphere.

'Way to go guys, burn up the dance floor,' called one.

'*Chak de phatte*,' shouted another, which had a much deeper historical meaning but for now just meant—be awesome. Typical busybodies thought Rohit, cheering from the sidelines but making no effort to join them on the dance floor and give them some moral support, which as if by some unseen signal had suddenly become empty.

Bowing formally, Renuka and Rohit put their arms on each other's shoulders, just as the band struck up another evergreen number, 'Congratulations' by Cliff Richard, which had bagged second place in the Eurovision Song Contest in 1968. As they started dancing, the awkwardness between them of the past few days melted away. It was not the first time that they had danced together. In their final term at the NDA, they were crowned Ms and Mr NDA, respectively. Then too, they had had to do a sort of victory dance, coincidentally, on this very same number. Then too, there had been similar words of jocular encouragement from the sidelines. From 'Hold her tighter' and '*Vyah kar lo* [get married]'—to '*Suhaag raat kithe* [where are the nuptials]?,' which had only added to their awkwardness. They had stumbled through the song, letting go of each other the moment the song got over, and returned to their respective squadron groups. Tonight was different though. The ambience was more serene, the assembled officers and ladies, perhaps sensing the chemistry between them, had fallen silent, mesmerized by the fluidity of their dancing. Looking deep into each other's eyes, they danced as if made for each other, their movements so in unison as if it were a practised choreography. Rohit was sorry when the number came to an end, and they closed with a dip. They stayed in that pose, Rohit clasping Renuka tightly around the waist, looking deep into each other's eyes a moment or two longer, as everyone clapped enthusiastically. The photographer must have taken a hundred photos and almost everyone had captured the dance on their mobile phones.

The party broke up into smaller groups, some to the bar to refill their glasses, some to sit in informal groups. A few of the couples also took the opportunity to walk around the lawns, appreciating the flower beds or making the short walk to the end of the lawn from where you could see the river glistening in the moonlight. There were some heated conversations too, as the discussions became more inebriated, voices louder than usual. The party was in full swing, showing no signs of winding down. The next day being a holiday, it was most likely that it would continue well past midnight.

The band struck up another number, a Punjabi one, and everyone was suddenly on the dance floor, gyrating wildly. The young officers were at the forefront of the dancing; finally a number they could dance to, which needed no partners. The band was also in the mood, belting out a medley of tunes one after the other without pause. Excusing himself, Rohit went to the bar to fetch himself a drink, a chilled beer to cool off after that heady dance. He glanced around for Renuka, but she was being fussed over by the other ladies, who were even more certain now that there was romance in the air, on the banks of the River Ganga—and that Rohit was the quintessential *chhora Ganga kinare wala*. The party was in full swing now, even Mota Singh and his wife were on the dance floor—he was surprisingly light on his feet and extremely gentle as he twirled his wife around. As there were no signs of dinner being served, Rohit decided to take a walk around the gardens to clear his head.

Involuntarily, his feet took him towards the rose garden. Rehmat and Rohit had been meeting in the seclusion of the rose garden on most evenings. He had told Rehmat that he would not be free this evening, but who knows, she might have sneaked in anyway, to have a peep at the party. It was already past ten and a most unlikely possibility, but the thought that she might just be there, a one-in-a-million chance, made him quicken his pace. Rohit sat down on a bench, 'their' bench as he contemplated the run of events of the last week. The train and road journey to Fatehpuri, Renuka his course-mate, travelling companion and dance partner, the nitty-gritty of regimental life, and to top it all, running into Rehmat, his childhood companion and the feelings between them. It was quite a heady mix of events and emotions. This last dance had only complicated matters; there was an inexplicable bond with Renuka too.

In his reverie, Rohit thought he spied some movement towards the gap in the boundary wall from where Rehmat normally came in. He tried to peer deeper but the lights from the lawns only deepened the shadows to this side. He was about to get up and rejoin the party when he saw a figure on the edge of the lawn walking on the pathway leading towards him. His first thought was that it might be Rehmat, but this was a sari-clad figure, definitely one of the ladies, walking slowly head down, and even from a distance, he could hear some faint sobs. He wondered what to do. Melt away in the darkness and rejoin the party or just keep sitting still, hoping that the lady would turn back? And who could it be? He tried to remember who he had met earlier in the evening and what they were wearing but it was too dark. He was about to get up and leave when he saw the lady hesitate and peer into the shadows, before letting out a blood-curdling scream. As she turned to run, a shadow leapt out of the darkness, knocking her to the ground, mauling her in the process, before bounding off over the boundary wall. Some of the officers nearby rushed in that direction. Rohit, after a moment's hesitation, also joined the group.

They came upon Anamika Chaddha, one of the married ladies and a former Miss India, who Mrs Menon was cradling in her lap. Drawing Anamika's sari pallu tightly around her, Mrs Menon asked, 'What happened? Are you all right? Who has done this to you?'

Anamika looked around with crazed, unfocused eyes at the sea of faces staring down at her, before settling her gaze on Rohit. Wordlessly, she pointed a trembling hand towards him, before falling into a dead faint. Everyone turned to look accusingly at Rohit who was shell-shocked. He tried to say something, but his throat had gone dry and words just wouldn't form.

All hell broke loose after that. Anamika was taken to the powder room of the Mess. The medical officer, Major Prabhu, who was also attending the party, shooed everyone out except for the commandant's wife. He gently turned Anamika over to tend to the wounds.

'Poor girl,' he said, 'just see those gashes on her back. It has ripped her blouse right off.' Anamika had been wearing a lowcut blouse with spaghetti straps, which was now in tatters. Anamika let out whimpering moans as Prabhu went about treating her wounds.

'I can't make out how she got these gashes. Looks like some sort of knife. But the parallel cuts are strange.'

'Just keep these observations to yourself for the time being,' instructed Mrs Menon. 'Let's not add more fuel to the fire.'

By now the ambulance had arrived and the patient was evacuated to the nearby military hospital. Lieutenant Colonel Mukesh Chaddha, Anamika's husband, sat beside her in the rear of the ambulance, gently patting her shoulder every time Anamika let out a terrified howl of pain.

The scene on the lawns was no less chaotic. Everyone was shell-shocked, huddled together in small groups. The married couples had gravitated towards each other, some holding hands, with husbands keeping a protective arm around their wives' shoulders. The young officers huddled in a group by themselves, with everyone looking accusingly at Rohit. Even Renuka was a little nonplussed. Rohit assaulting a woman? Unbelievable! Major Vikrant, the adjutant, was trying to get some semblance of control, clearing a path from the rose garden to the Mess building, instructing the stewards to stay back and asking everyone to stay calm. The jolliness of the evening had gone, as were any thoughts of dinner.

'I had told you to keep an eye on Rohit,' said the commandant, calling Vikrant to his side. 'Now see what he has gone and done. Take him away from here, under escort. Tell his room partner to keep an eye on him. He is confined to lines and not to go out anywhere without my say-so.'

A chastened Vikrant turned away to carry out this unpleasant order. Though bewildered at this sudden turn of events, Rohit took it all stoically. As he was being led away, Moti Singh turned towards his wife and said in a voice loud enough for everyone to hear, '*Main twannu dasiya si, aa munda gaddari hega* [I had told you this boy is a trouble-maker].'

And on that note, the evening ended abruptly. Nobody gave a second glance towards the rose garden, where trampled underfoot, unnoticed in the general confusion lay the remnants of a green rose.

Chapter 4

Inquiry

The mood in the garrison the next day was quite sombre. Word had got out regarding the unusual happenings of the night before. Wild parties were not unknown, but a woman being assaulted in the Mess premises was unimaginable. That too when a party was in progress. The senior officers and ladies met in the commandant's house to discuss the next course of action. The deputy commandant, Colonel Ravindran and his wife Mona, and the training battalion commander, Colonel Ramesh Anand and his wife Bina were present.

Brigadier Menon opened by asking, 'How's the lady doing? Any fresh update since last night?'

Colonel Ravindran replied, 'She's stable. Still in a bit of shock, so she's been sedated. The nature of the injuries is still unknown but they are not life-threatening.'

The deputy was an experienced soldier who had seen action as a young officer in the Kargil War. He was not one to get jittery or overreact. 'What has happened is indeed sad,' he added. 'But we need to keep rumours from spreading. Also, we need to get at the bottom of this incident and take stringent action against all those found guilty.'

'That's true,' said Colonel Anand, 'but we also must keep the reputation of the Regiment in mind. It's best if we hush up the matter, have an internal inquiry and dispose of the case under your powers.' This last bit was addressed to the commandant, who had the powers to try minor misdemeanours.

The ladies present were quite agitated by this suggestion. 'How can you say that?' said Mona, 'A woman has been assaulted right in front of us, her modesty outraged. And you just want to let the culprit off?'

Priya, the commandant's wife, was similarly affronted, 'Regimental honour cannot supplant natural justice. When will you guys get out of this feudalistic mindset?'

'That's not what I meant,' backtracked Anand. 'If we want to give Rohit some bigger punishment, then it means trial by court martial. Everyone will come to know. Rohit is a third-generation officer, his father is a three-star general.

Just imagine the damage to their reputations. Let's deal with it within ourselves.'

'What about her reputation?' chimed in the ladies. 'We must have a proper investigation, or our ladies will never feel safe again.'

The discussion ranged back and forth. Another round of tea was served. The staff knew that something was amiss and went about their duties in a subdued manner. Brigadier Menon sat silently, listening to all the various arguments with only half a ear, mentally examining and discarding various options. There certainly must be an inquiry, but at what level? What if something like this had happened to their own daughter? Would they have kept quiet or gone straight to the police?

During a lull in the conversation, he held up his hand, to signal them to stop speaking. Without realizing it, their tempers had frayed, their voices raised as they argued with each other. There seemed to be two camps. One comprised the deputy and the ladies wanting stringent action, and the other Anand, the lone dissenter.

'Please stop and listen to me,' said the commandant, and proceeded to outline his argument. 'There is no doubt that we must get to the bottom of this case. There is no question of hushing it up. At the same time, we must give Rohit a fair chance, too. We cannot presuppose his guilt and for that to happen, we need to have a proper inquiry.'

Turning to the deputy commandant he added, 'Please convene an inquiry headed by the staff officer training, Lieutenant Colonel Varinder Kumar, with members from the staff of the Centre. Since there is a lady involved, include Renuka too as one of the members. I'll ring up the area commander in the evening to update him. Meanwhile, let a preliminary written report go through official channels. There should not be any feeling that we are trying to hush up the issue.'

With matters under control at least for the time being, they broke off to spend what remained of the day in their various duties. On his way back to his residence, the training battalion commander decided to detour via the officers' quarters to see how the youngsters were coping with the previous evening's events. Colonel Anand found them sitting in a group in the living area. It was a sparsely furnished room, more like a waiting room with a sofa set and a couple of chairs, with a TV on one wall tuned to one of the many news channels. Cups of tea and the remnants of a plate of biscuits lay scattered about. A centre table held a flower vase with some wilted flowers, which resembled the mood in the room.

The officers had been having a discussion of their own, no less heated than the one in the commandant's home. 'What the hell were you thinking?' said Naresh to Rohit. 'After giving us a long lecture about behaving ourselves, you're the one who went and misbehaved with that lady.'

'I haven't done anything!' remonstrated Rohit. 'I'm as surprised and shocked as the rest of you.'

'Then what were you doing all alone in the rose garden?' added Sarmah. 'Surely you were there for some reason?'

Rohit was hard-pressed to answer, as he did not want to drag Rehmat into the picture. At the same time, his silence only strengthened their suspicions. *It's strange* thought Rohit, *my own course-mates are disowning me.*

Renuka was silent through all these exchanges. She was as shocked as the others. Rohit assaulting a woman? No way. Not after the way he had risen to her defence. Not only her defence, but that of women. This is not the Rohit she knew. Not her Rohit. And certainly not after that electrifying dance. Staring into the distance, she was the first to notice Colonel Anand coming towards the living room. 'Attention!' she said, rising crisply to her feet, with the others following suit.

'What's up, guys?' he asked informally and noticing Renuka, he added, 'Guys and gals?' Sitting down on one of the seats that had been hastily vacated for him, he continued, after being handed a cup of tea, 'Why so glum and morose? What's happened has happened. That cannot be undone, so now we must move ahead.'

'Ahead how?' blurted Rohit. 'Everyone here believes I'm to blame. Surely you don't think so too, Sir?'

Colonel Anand looked at Rohit and paused before answering. He could tell Rohit was under strain. The poise and self-assurance of the last few days were missing, the swagger gone. 'First the good news. Mrs Chaddha is in hospital and resting. Her injuries are serious but not life-threatening. So that's one less thing to worry about.'

They all let out a collective sigh of relief, but continued to look questioningly at their senior . . . what was the bad news going to be?

'An incident like this cannot be brushed aside. I have just come from the commandant's house where we had a long discussion. A formal inquiry will be held, official cognizance taken of an untoward happening on army premises. The presiding officer will be the staff officer training, and Renuka will be one of the members of the inquiry.'

This last part jolted Renuka out of her reverie. 'Why me? I'm such a junior officer and have no experience.'

'You'll only gain experience by doing things. There's always a first time. Moreover, since a lady is involved, it is mandatory to have a woman member. Since you're the only woman officer, it must be you.' Putting down his teacup, he rose to leave the room, adding, 'I'll send the convening order by this evening. The Court should assemble first thing in the morning. At best, it should conclude in a couple of days.'

The officers looked at each other wordlessly, each lost in their own thoughts. Rohit was the most devastated. A Court of Inquiry against him! A third-generation officer, whose father and grandfather had fought in all the wars since Independence. His father would throw a fit. *Better that he should hear it from me*, thought Rohit, and excusing himself, left the room.

'Hi Dad,' said Rohit when his father answered his call. 'There's been a bit of an incident yesterday in the Centre.'

'Yes, I came to know about it,' replied his father. 'The commandant gave me a call. He didn't have to, but I suppose he did it out of courtesy to a former commandant. Now tell me, son, what's this all about?'

Rohit briefly gave his recollection of events. 'A Court of Inquiry has been ordered against me, but I tell you Dad, I had nothing to do with it.'

'I believe you, *beta*, do you want me to do something?'

Rohit thought for a while before replying, 'No Dad, let it be for the time being. Your saying or doing anything at this juncture will be misconstrued.'

'That's my boy,' replied his father. 'I expected nothing less from you. Chest out, chin up.'

Renuka had mixed feelings. She did not want to be part of any inquiry so early in her career. On one side was the institution, the great Indian Army, and on the other, a newly commissioned young officer. Whose side should she take? And did she want to be part of the Court that could end a budding career? Who could she possibly confide in? The only person who came to mind was Mrs Moti Singh, who had made her feel so welcome on the evening of the party, an evening that would forever remain etched in her memory. The romantic ambience of a star-studded night on the banks of the Ganga harshly interrupted by screams from the rose garden; Anamika running back towards the lawn with a terrified look, holding on to her tattered dress; Rohit running behind Anamika from the same direction; and the way Anamika had pointed towards Rohit before losing consciousness. It all added up to a dismal picture.

The other officers all went their different ways, somewhat relieved that they were off the hook, not involved in any manner. Some of them had been a bit boisterous the previous evening, even flirting with the younger ladies and they had been worried that their actions might also come under the scanner. They went off to the Mess for lunch, where there were no signs of the previous evening's festivities. Everything was back to normal, including the statues of the two malis toiling motionlessly under the afternoon sun. The inside of the Mess was all cleaned up too, with one of the staff giving some finishing touches, brushing the trophies with a feather duster. Entering the anteroom, the officers glanced around at all the glittering silver pieces and objets d'art, before moving towards the bar, where they were welcomed as usual by the guardian Tendu, one muddied paw raised menacingly in the air.

* * *

The next morning all the members of the Court assembled in the staff officer training's office. Apart from Lt Col Varinder Kumar, whose office it was and who was to be the presiding officer, also present were Renuka and Captain Som Jha, an officer from the Records office, the third member of the Court, as nominated in the convening order. Jha had originally been a clerk in the same Regiment, but then applied for a regimental commission and was now an officer in the Records Branch. Quite content with having become an officer, he had no further ambitions, except to earn his pension.

'All in?' asked Colonel Varinder. When both nodded in the affirmative, he continued, 'The Court will function from the officers' study room, and we'll go there shortly. But before that, follow me to the deputy commandant's office as he would like to brief us first.'

Colonel Ravindran was seated at his desk in his office, making some notes, a pile of files on one side waiting to be cleared. The deputy had a rugged but handsome look, nose slightly askew, a reminder of his boxing days. As a young officer, he had seen action in the Kargil War. 'Please sit down. Just give me a minute,' he said.

While waiting for him to finish, Renuka looked around. Behind the desk was the usual appointment board giving the names and tenures of all the past incumbents. The names dated back to pre-Independence days, with British names giving way gradually to Indian names. Most of the names were unfamiliar, but she did see the name of one former army chief. Silver trophies and mementos lined one wall, a testimony to the various competitions won by the Centre.

Heaving a sigh, Ravindran looked up at the trio seated in front of him. Taking a sip of tea, he began, 'This is an awkward inquiry, particularly since an officer's wife is involved. You all have a copy of the convening order, I hope?'

'Yes, Sir,' they replied.

'Well, I would like the inquiry to be conducted with the minimum fuss and in the shortest possible time. No need to get into too many details. What is the purpose of the inquiry?' He looked at Jha, who squirmed in his seat.

Seeing that, Renuka butted in, 'The purpose of an inquiry is to ascertain whether, prima facie, there is any cause to proceed with further disciplinary proceedings,' which only resulted in a furious glare from Jha.

'That's right,' said Colonel Ravindran, pleasantly surprised but also a bit taken aback as the most important point of his briefing had been dealt with by this young girl. 'Yours is basically a fact-finding mission, and your recommendations are only a guide for the convening authority, in this case the commandant, to decide the further course of action. Accordingly, limit yourself to the matter at hand. Any questions?' Not expecting any, and seeing Varinder get to his feet, he turned towards his files.

'Just one doubt, Sir,' said Renuka, hesitatingly raising her hand. 'You said that this is only a preliminary inquiry, yet the wording of the convening order is putting the onus on Rohit to prove his innocence. I think the language needs to be changed.'

The deputy commandant sighed once again, this time in exasperation. 'What do you mean?' he asked, hoping she was not going to be a pain in the neck in her youthful exuberance. Or was it because they were course-mates? Or something more—if last night's dance was anything to go by?

'Well, Lieutenant Rohit should not be mentioned by name in the convening order. Our inquiry should only be to ascertain the events of last evening leading to a lady being assaulted. Let the inquiry bring out who is to blame,' Renuka replied.

'It seems we have a budding lawyer among us, not an infantry officer,' said Ravindran, slightly irritated by her impertinence and adding sarcastically. 'Why don't you draft a fresh order as per your liking? Out now! Varinder, come back with a fresh draft.' And this time, he picked up a file and thumped it on his desk to show that the meeting was over.

'What is wrong with you, Renuka?' asked Varinder once they were back in his office. 'The deputy is twice your age, almost like your father, and you were questioning him? You're starting your army career on the wrong foot.'

'With due respect, Sir, aren't we supposed to be impartial? Even before the inquiry has begun, we are jumping to conclusions.'

'Don't take it so seriously,' advised Jha. 'I've done many such inquiries. Let's not unnecessarily get bogged down. I'm slated to go on leave this Friday, so let's wrap it up quickly.'

Renuka meanwhile had furiously scribbled a fresh draft with many deletions and over-writings, which she handed over to Varinder, who turned to his computer, keyed in the draft and, after a quick check, forwarded it through the LAN to the deputy.

As expected, the intercom buzzed a few moments later. 'Please come to my office,' said Ravindran, and Varinder rose to go.

'Wait for me here,' he said. 'And remember, not a word to anybody. All our deliberations are confidential.'

Motioning Varinder to sit down, the deputy said, 'I hope this girl is not going to create problems for us. I've seen this fresh draft, and you can issue it, but it will mean more diligence on the part of the Court to pin-point culpability.'

'Don't worry, Sir. I'll handle it. There are hardly any witnesses; it's an open-and-shut case. I'll have it wrapped up in no time.'

'Please do that, but remember, I don't want any scandal or anything else that would besmirch the reputation of the Regiment. Keep it low-key and above all, keep that pipsqueak under control.'

Varinder smiled as he saluted and turned to go. Renuka really seemed to have got on the deputy's nerves. Unfazed in front of enemy fire, but unnerved by a young woman officer, this was uncharted territory for him. It was tough to deal with women in the ranks. One didn't know whether to treat them as officers or as ladies.

Returning to his office, he informed the other members to break off for the time being. 'I have other work to attend to. I'll issue a fresh convening order by the evening, and we will assemble in the study room at 0800 hours sharp tomorrow morning.'

'Right, Sir,' said Jha and Renuka in unison, and retreated to the adjutant's office to see if there were any other orders for the day. 'Nothing for the two of you. You are relieved of all your other duties from now on till the inquiry is complete. That doesn't mean you can take your time.' Turning to Jha, he smiled and added, 'Remember your leave depends on finishing this soonest.'

At this, Jha scowled once again at Renuka. The whole day wasted because of her, when they could have easily been halfway through the inquiry. Rohit and Renuka and the whole world be damned, his leave was more important. From tomorrow onwards, he vowed to himself as he stormed out, I'll make sure that things proceed expeditiously without allowing Renuka to stymie the proceedings, and spoil his leave plans.

* * *

Renuka went by herself to the Mess where the other officers had already reached after the day's training. All of them were anxious to know what had transpired. Renuka brought them up to date.

'That was smart of you to get the convening order changed,' said Naresh. 'I would have never thought of it.'

'How could you have? You slept through all the classes on military law,' said Sarmah, punching him on the shoulder. Sarmah was the brainy one, with a CGPA one could only dream of. Renuka looked at Rohit, expecting him to say something.

'Thanks, Renuka, but let it be. I just want the inquiry to get over so that we can move on and report to our units.'

'How can you be so cool?' she shot back. 'You must fight it out. I know you couldn't have done anything so ghastly. If you don't protest, everyone will think you are guilty.'

'Well, that's a cross I'll have to bear. What can I say against a lady? It will be her word against mine. It's not only me but my family's reputation that is at stake. The more the inquiry drags on, the more the damage. So let it be.'

Renuka was not entirely convinced but hearing Rohit's despondent voice and seeing his drooping shoulders, she wisely kept quiet. She wanted to give him a reassuring hug, a *jadoo ki jhappi*, but she refrained from doing so, afraid of being rebuffed and unsure of how it would seem to the others.

* * *

The Court assembled the next day in the study room, where the furniture had been rearranged for the purpose of the inquiry. On one end of the room, three tables had been joined end to end and covered with a green cloth, where the presiding officer and members would sit. In front of that was a single chair for the witnesses, who would be called in one by one to give their testimony. Witnesses were not sworn in as such, but once their testimony had been converted in writing, they had to sign to say that their testimony had been correctly recorded.

Lieutenant Colonel Varinder took his place in the centre, flanked by the other two members, Jha to his right and Renuka to his left. At each seat was a pen stand with assorted stationery items—pencils, erasers, paper clips, a clipboard and the like. In front of the presiding officer were also placed two thick volumes of the Manual of Military Law, should the need to consult it arise.

'All set?' asked Varinder. 'I have made a list of probable witnesses, who we shall call one by one, starting with Mrs Chaddha. Remember she has been through a traumatic experience, so let's not trouble her too much. Renuka, you should take down the statements in point form. After each witness has given their statement, we will write it in fair, show it to them, and get their signatures before letting them go.'

'That's a good idea,' said Jha. 'Not only will it speed up the process, but the witnesses will not be able to change their statements later.'

'Who do you propose to call, Sir?' asked Renuka, adjusting the various items placed in front of her.

'Well. I thought we could start with Anamika, followed by the medical officer. Moti Singh and perhaps one or two officers to corroborate any facts that come out.'

'And what about Rohit? Don't we need to take his statement too?'

'Yes, of course, but I'm keeping him for the last.'

'Correct, Sir,' said Jha, thinking about his scheduled leave. 'We will be able to nail him down when he gives his statement and close the inquiry. Another day to summarize the findings and we should be done by Wednesday at the latest.'

Pressing the buzzer that lay in front of him, he instructed the runner to summon Anamika from the waiting room. The officers got to their feet when she entered and Varinder requested her to sit. Anamika looked quite different today. She still had a few bruises on her face, and she winced in pain while sitting down. She was simply dressed in an off-white salwar kurta, with just a hint of make-up. Even then, there was no mistaking her inherent beauty. That men would be attracted to her and might go to any lengths to pursue her was understandable though undesirable.

'Good morning, Mrs Chadha,' began Varinder formally. 'We are all sorry for what happened and equally sorry for having to call you here, but it can't be helped. We'll try to be as quick as possible. If you're ready, we can begin.'

'What would you like to know? Will you be asking me questions?'

'Just describe in your own words the events of that evening. Renuka here will take down notes and convert it into a formal statement for you to sign. Take your time and begin when you're ready.'

Anamika sat for a moment with her head bowed. Noticing a glass of water on the side table beside her, she took a small sip and commenced speaking. 'Nothing much to say, really. The party was in full swing. I had spoken to several ladies and officers, even some of the young officers, and needed a break, so I went towards the rose garden. I thought I heard some footsteps behind me, and supposed it was one of the young officers, Sarmah perhaps, who had been flirting with me. Just as I looked over my shoulder somebody shoved me in the back and ripped my blouse off. I stumbled and almost fell but somehow managed to keep my footing and screaming for help, I ran back towards the lawn. The next thing I knew I was in the back of the ambulance taking me to the military hospital.'

'Do you remember anything else, ma'am? Any idea who did this to you? Any enemies or maybe someone jealous of you?'

Anamika looked at Varinder for a while and exchanged a meaningful look. 'No, not that I can think off. We have only been recently married and are new to the station.'

Smiling ruefully she added, 'Not enough time to make any enemies.'

'Som? Renuka? Any questions?' Jha shook his head, but Renuka said she would like to ask a few questions.

'You cannot say who attacked you, but why did you point to Rohit?'

'Many people have been asking me the same question and I really don't know why. I do believe I saw him sitting on a bench a little down the path. Maybe that's what remained in my subconscious before I passed out.'

Renuka paused for a while before continuing. 'We were all there, ma'am, and heard your terrible screams, what scared you so much? And the injuries—deep gashes down your whole back . . . surely it was not Rohit who did that?'

'I have said what I had to say. There's nothing more to add. Why are you cross-questioning me as if I am at fault?' Turning to Varinder, she asked, 'Can I go now? You promised.'

Varinder nodded his assent and was rewarded by a warm look. 'Please wait in my office. Have a cup of tea. I'll call you later to take your signature.' They all stood up as Anamika left the room.

'What's wrong with you, Renuka? Hassling the poor girl. Just quickly prepare her statement and get it to me.

We'll take a short break till then. Som, keep our next witness ready.'

'But Sir,' said Renuka, relentlessly like a dog with a bone, if she is indeed accusing Rohit, then he has a right to defend himself.'

That's true, thought Varinder, the army rules expressly clarified that whenever anybody's character or military reputation was at stake, then that person had a right to be present throughout the hearing. 'All right, all right. Write out the statement and when we re-assemble, make sure Rohit is present. I'm not sure what more he can ask, but we will go by the book.'

When they reassembled, Renuka read out Anamika's statement and asked her if it matched what she had said. 'Are you sure, ma'am? And do you still maintain that Rohit is not beyond suspicion?'

'Why? Are you accusing me of lying?' retorted Anamika. 'Instead of catching the bastard who did this to me, you are wasting your time in this futile inquiry.'

'Keep calm, ma'am,' interjected Varinder solicitously. 'It's just that we must follow due process. If you still feel Rohit is somehow involved, then I must give him the opportunity to defend himself. Otherwise, there is no case at all.'

'Call him then. Let him see for himself what has been said.'

Rohit entered the room, saluted and on being instructed to, sat down on another chair that had been placed a little away and at a right angle to the witness chair. Anamika's statement was read out once again and Varinder explained patiently the import of the statement. 'As per army rules, you are at liberty to ask questions of this and any subsequent witnesses. Do you want to ask any questions?'

Rohit looked a bit anxious, was he now the accused who had to prove his innocence? Till yesterday everything seemed low-key, and now he was being painted as a sexual offender. He groaned and put his face in his hands. 'Nothing to say and nothing to ask,' he replied. 'If she says that's what happened, then that's what happened. I will not question the word of a lady.' That took everyone by surprise. Varinder had anticipated another round of acrimonious questioning and was glad that this witness was done with. The others would be much faster and simpler in comparison.

* * *

Renuka was quite taken aback at Rohit's refusal to defend himself. She would have to fight on his behalf.

Her thoughts were interrupted by the entrance of the next witness, the medical officer who had treated Anamika. After exchanging courtesies and preliminaries, he was asked to give his version of the events.

'I was at the party like everyone else,' he began. 'I was at the other end of the lawn when I heard screams coming from the direction of the rose garden. After a little while, I heard voices calling, "Fetch the doctor; where's Prabhu, he was around here only" and so on. I went towards the sound of the commotion where the officers and ladies were gathered. When I pushed forward, I saw Anamika ma'am lying on the ground with her head cradled on the commandant ma'am's lap. There were some bruise marks on her face, but she was moaning as if in great pain. With the help of a few of the staff, we carried her into the ladies' room where I could examine her better.'

'And what did you see?' asked Varinder.

'Well, Anamika was unconscious by then and only the commandant's wife and I were in the room. We had placed her on the ground as there were no tables and blood had already stained the carpet. I gently turned her around and was shocked. Her entire back had deep gashes on it. Almost vertical, deeper on top. Her blouse was torn to shreds.

She needed proper medical care, so I just put a light dressing on the wounds before taking her in the ambulance to the hospital.'

'Any thoughts on what might have caused the injuries?' asked Renuka, thinking that it surely would have taken some time for someone to stab Anamika three or four times.

'It's strange that you should ask that,' answered Prabhu. 'The injuries were not stabs but more like gashes almost parallel to each other. There were also bits of leaves and petals and some dirt in the gashes, but that must have come from when she was lying on the lawn.'

'Did she say anything at all during this time?' Prabhu hesitated a while before answering, glancing briefly towards Rohit.

'Not really, except for two words.'

'And what were they?' asked Varinder irritably. 'You don't have to hide anything.'

'Just "monster" and "Rohit". In fact, she repeated these two words several times in her delirious state.'

Everyone turned to look at Rohit, who was shell-shocked, mouth agape and an unbelieving look in his eyes. *Surely Rohit will challenge this statement at least*, thought Renuka. But when given an opportunity to question the doctor, Rohit once again sat silently, with a defeated demeanour. It was as if he had given up.

'I guess that's enough for today,' said Varinder, once they were alone. 'Two witnesses have positively identified Rohit, who is not denying anything. Just one or two more witnesses and finally Rohit's statement, and we should be done.'

Renuka, though, was not going to give in so easily. 'How do you explain the injuries, Sir? And what motive could Rohit possibly have? Nobody has said that they saw the two of them together, or Rohit actually striking her. I think we are jumping to conclusions.'

'Nobody is jumping to anything,' retorted Varinder coldly. 'Mind your tone, young girl. Nobody outrages the modesty of a lady or assaults anyone in full view. That would be obvious to everyone except someone blinded by love.'

It was now Renuka who stood speechless, with Captain Som Jha smirking in the background, happy that at last Renuka had been put in her place. Army hierarchy must be respected after all. One couldn't possibly have juniors, that too recently commissioned ones, questioning their seniors.

Chapter 5

Surprises Galore

Renuka returned to her room in a state of confusion. What did Varinder mean by saying love had blinded her? She was just trying to do her job to see that justice was done. Everyone is innocent until proven guilty was the maxim and that's exactly what she was doing and would have done so irrespective of the people involved. On the spur of the moment, she decided to look up Anamika who had gone back to the hospital to recuperate. The hospital lay en route to the Mess, in a little walled-up compound of its own. Large, centuries-old trees with thick leafy canopies offered a lot of shade, which was a boon during the hot summer months. The wards were in long barracks that looked as old as the trees, with sloping corrugated steel roofs and the odd shoot sprouting from the walls where some seed had taken root. The officers' family ward was in one such barracks, with a verandah running along its entire length from which the rooms could be accessed.

After inquiring from the nurse on duty, Renuka went to Anamika's room. There were two beds in each room but fortunately Anamika was the sole occupant in hers. She was lying on her stomach, head raised up, watching some programme on the TV. The bed and other furniture, all in steel painted white, gave the room a depressing look.

'How are you feeling now?' inquired Renuka.

'A bit better, thanks. But what are you doing here? I've already given my statement to the Court.'

'I just thought I'd look you up. Prabhu, the doctor, said something that I wanted to check out.'

'What did he say? Will I have to come again to depose? I'm just not in the mood for that. It's been a horrible experience.'

'Yes, I can understand. And that's why I want to get to the bottom of this. Prabhu mentioned that in your delirium, you kept saying "monster" and "Rohit". What was that about, do you remember?'

Anamika gave a shudder and a terrified look crossed her face. Renuka put her arm around Anamika. 'Don't worry, you are safe now. Nobody can touch you here.'

Looking searchingly at Renuka, she replied, 'I really don't know. It's just images flashing before my eyes. I had glanced over my shoulder, as I mentioned in my statement and when I looked forward again there was this monstrous face right in front of me. I turned to run and that's when I felt a burning pain on my back. Whatever it was, it snagged on my blouse. The moment it snapped I got thrown forward and fell on my face. I had looked back once while running and that's when I saw Rohit running towards me.'

Renuka took a moment to digest this new information before asking, 'Then why did you point towards Rohit? He was too far away to have done this.'

'I don't know, I don't know. This is just too horrible. A nightmare. I think what I was trying to indicate was that Rohit might have seen something, and he would shed some light on what happened. I didn't think it would implicate him. Why doesn't he say something to clear his own name?'

'This gives a totally new complexion to the case. You must give an additional statement. Rohit is too much of a gentleman to challenge your word.'

'Must I? Every time I talk about it, I get the shivers.'

Renuka took Anamika's hands in hers. 'Please,' she pleaded, 'for Rohit's sake.'

'You're very much in love with him, aren't you?'

Renuka was taken back for the second time that day. *Was it so obvious?*

'Nothing like that. He's a course-mate and moreover, it is my duty as a member of the Court.'

Anamika rolled her eyes and smiled, her first in many days. 'Oh, you silly girl. You can't hide your feelings from me. I'll do as you say, not just for Rohit but for both your sakes.'

* * *

After lunch, they returned to the officers' quarters and gathered in the lounge. The officers had wanted to know everything, but Renuka did not want to talk in front of the Mess staff. She brought them up to date but did not tell them of her impromptu visit to the hospital. Sarmah squirmed a bit when the part about him flirting with Anamika came up. 'Hey, all of you were flirting with her too.'

'Maybe, but you were the only one looking at her with puppy eyes,' said Renuka.

'What rubbish,' said Sarmah before storming out. One by one they all left to go to their respective rooms till only Renuka and Rohit were left. Once she was certain that they were alone, she sat down on the sofa next to him and told him in a low voice about her talk with Anamika, leaving out the last part. 'She is willing to give an additional statement. Don't give up so easily.'

Rohit placed a hand on hers, giving it a little supportive shake, but not removing it. 'You worry too much, Renu,' he said, using her pet name. 'The truth will come out in due course. I'm innocent. I haven't done anything, I just happened to be there, that's all.'

'Yes, but then why were you there all by yourself? You're acting so mysteriously and that's why everyone suspects you.'

To that, Rohit just shrugged as if to say, 'So be it.' That really infuriated Renuka and snatching her hand away from under Rohit's, she stormed out of the room, leaving Rohit immersed in his thoughts.

He was still sitting there when the photographer came with the photos and videos of the party. Rohit asked him to call all the others too, and they turned up one by one, in shorts and T-shirts or track suits, and they were surprised to see him still in uniform. 'What's up, boss? Why are you still in uniform?'

'Ah, just like that. I thought the Court may assemble again so I didn't feel like changing. Anyway, settle down and let's look at our dining-in pictures. Why don't we order some tea?'

Meanwhile, the photographer had hooked up his laptop to the wall-mounted TV and soon opened the first file showing their arrival at the Mess and being received by the commandant. There were dozens and dozens of photos taken from all angles, sometimes catching them in awkward poses, which brought out peals of laughter and sarcastic comments. The photographer then showed some videos of the event and the video of Renuka and Rohit dancing was definitely the best part. '*Wah wah*!' exclaimed everyone. 'We must have a jam session again.' Rohit glanced at Renuka, and their eyes met. He blew her a flying kiss much to the amusement of the others, which Renuka, not to be outdone caught and blew right back. Everyone laughed joyously, the tension of the previous couple of days forgotten. This was the Rohit of old.

The photographer left soon after, leaving a copy of the photos on a pen drive. 'You can see it again at leisure. Just write down the number of the pics that you want, and I'll print them out for you.'

They went their own ways after that, with Renuka retaining the pen drive for viewing. After dinner, changing into a nightie, she powered up her laptop, inserted the pen drive and copied the files to her desktop. Quickly checking and replying to a couple of emails, she started to view the photos. The pics were indeed of a professional quality and the photographer had done a good job of catching everyone, not just them, in the most casual moments. As she was doing so, a thought struck her, and she went back and forth between the pics. Excited by her findings, she opened a separate folder and quickly copied a few of the selected pics there. Slipping on her dressing gown, she went and knocked on Rohit's door.

'Come with me, I need to show you something,' she said, when he opened the door and before he could react, took his hand and dragged him back to her room.

'What are you doing, Renu? You know it's inappropriate for me to be here.'

'Just shut up and sit at the table. You couldn't possibly be in any more trouble than you are now.'

'Leave the front door open,' commanded Rohit. 'I don't want to be in deeper trouble.'

'Ah, scared to be alone in the same room with me, is it?' Nevertheless, she did leave the door ajar, the rusty hinges squeaking as the door swayed in the breeze.

'What did you want to show me?' asked Rohit once they were seated at the study table, shoulders touching, heads close to each other.

'Look carefully at all these photos I have segregated and tell me what you see.' Rohit went through the dozen or so photos. All he could see were a bunch of officers enjoying themselves. The ladies looked beautiful in the many-coloured saris and even he paused a little longer on the shots where Anamika was the centre of attraction.

'Stop ogling and tell me what you see.' Rohit couldn't fathom why Renuka had roused him out of bed to see a bunch of photos he had seen earlier in the evening.

'Why don't you tell me? It's late. Along with mine, your reputation will also go down the drain.'

'See here in the background. Do you see the malis sitting there?'

'Yes, so what's so great about that? They are a permanent fixture of the Officers' Mess. You were the only one to comment about them, and I had told you that they were statues, the first day we went to the Mess, remember?'

'Then can you explain how there are two malis in this pic? And again two malis in this pic, that too in a different place? Or how there is only one statue where there were two earlier? Have the malis suddenly come to life?'

Rohit suddenly sat up straighter as he realized the import of what he had just seen. Impulsively, he turned and gave Renuka a quick peck on the cheek.

'We need to check this out further. Who could this mysterious third person be? Let's have a look at the video clips, there might be something there too.'

They viewed the clips one by one. They lingered over the one of them dancing and involuntarily their hands intertwined. Renuka nudged Rohit out of his reverie. 'Look for the mali,' she said. 'Stop looking at me.'

Rohit grinned and gave her another peck on the cheek. 'Why should I look at your pics when you're sitting right next to me?' Renuka beamed and held Rohit's chin, turning his head back to the screen.

'Run this part again,' she said. 'See this person crouching in the background and going towards the rose garden. He must be the one who attacked Anamika. We must bring this to the notice of the Court.' Pleased at her own detective skills, she threw her arms around Rohit and gave him a resounding kiss.

* * *

The next morning when the Court assembled, Renuka showed Varinder her findings. Som was not impressed.

'This does not prove anything,' he said. 'How do we even know that the photos and videos are genuine? Renuka is trying to delay the proceedings.'

Varinder looked thoughtfully at the screen, clicking back and forth between the photos. 'Well,' he said at last, 'firstly, we will have to call the photographer and take his statement, and he will have to introduce the photos and videos as evidence.' Pointing at Renuka, he added, 'We can't be having you as a member doing that. Only after that can you then bring out the inconsistencies you have told us. Let us follow the correct procedure.'

'Send for the photographer,' he instructed Jha, 'and till he comes, we will adjourn, while I brief the commandant of these latest developments.'

The photographer was called, and his statement taken. When shown the photos in question he was as taken aback as everyone else. 'I really hadn't looked at them so closely, I was concentrating on the young officers as they were the guests. But now that you mention it, there are a few more photos that you should see.' He quickly turned towards the laptop and with a few quick clicks, dragged another set of photos into a temporary folder. 'See here,' he said, 'in this pic you can see Anamika and her husband arguing about something. In the video, it is after this argument that she walks off to the rose garden, and her husband is nowhere to be seen till after the attack. And in this set, you can see Jeevan, the Mess in-charge lurking about, often eavesdropping, especially around the ladies. See here, in this one he has his arm around this young girl.'

'I think it is Major Bahadur's daughter Roma,' interjected Varinder. 'This just won't do, why didn't you tell us any of this before?'

'Sahib, Jeevan has been around for donkey's years. Right from the time when Rohit's father was the commandant. Who would have believed me? Besides, all of you were at the party, surely you noticed his behaviour? If none of you saw anything amiss, who am I to butt in? I'm just small fry.'

'Let's leave Jeevan out for the time being and get to the bottom of this mali business,' said Varinder. 'I think a visit to the Mess is called for. Get the cars ready and ask the Mess secretary to be present. He should also assemble all the staff, including the malis.'

They all drove to the Mess. Renuka and Rohit sat together in the back of one of the SUVs while Varinder sat in front. On reaching the Mess, they tried to re-create the scene of the party, with Renuka and Rohit standing near the dance floor. The statues of the malis were in another part of the lawn, and had probably been moved since.

'See here,' said Renuka, pointing to a dried-up portion of the lawn. 'This is where the statues were the day of the party, the grass below is dried up. But here there is only one patch, whereas the pics show two.' Moving to another part of the lawn, she again pointed out the same anomaly. 'One dried-up patch but two malis in the pic.'

'What does that mean?' asked Lieutenant Colonel Chaddha, the Mess secretary. It was his wife who had been assaulted and he was naturally worried.

'I think the statues were kept singly and this third mysterious person was sitting beside each of the statues in turn. We are so used to seeing two malis sitting together that none of us gave it a second thought. I guess we need to talk to the malis,' said Varinder turning to Jeevan, the head butler. 'Get all of them here. Time to question them a bit.'

Jeevan turned to go, and Renuka thought he looked a bit worried, but it was just a fleeting glimpse. Perhaps he was just upset that something like this had happened on his watch.

The malis were called and they all stood silently, staring sullenly at the ground. They had no explanation for where and why the statues had been moved.

'Who oversees the statues?' asked Varinder. 'Who moves them from one place to the other?'

'*Ji*, sahib, that would be me,' said Dhani Ram. 'I move the statues from place to place every three to four days so that the lawn does not get spoiled. They are quite heavy and I normally take the help of another mali.'

'Where were they on the day of the party?'

'They were adjacent to the stage; I had moved them there earlier in the week.'

'That's why there were two marks, but then what about the other place, where there were two malis in the pic again?'

'I don't know,' said Dhani Ram. 'This is where I had kept the statues and that's where they were when we left when our duty was over. That was about five o'clock in the evening, and there were many people here preparing for the party. Maybe someone from the working party moved the statues?'

'See here,' said Rohit, 'and tell me if I am mistaken. The dried-up patches here are older and yellower, where the statues were kept earlier. At the second place, the patch is still green. So, someone moved just one statue to a new location. Someone who had an ulterior motive. Sometime after the malis had left and before the party started. It must be an old hand who nobody would think twice about. We should question everyone from the working party.'

This is getting more and more complicated, thought Varinder. What seemed to be an open-and-shut case had been blown wide open. Perhaps they had been wrong to pre-judge Rohit or to question Renuka's motives to ensure a free and fair inquiry.

'Tell the adjutant, Vikrant, to find out the details of that day's working parties. I want the JCO in-charge and the entire working party in the office quadrangle first thing in the morning. They are excused from the first period.'

* * *

The recruits were all fallen-in as per their respective companies for the morning physical training period. They were all in their PT rig—khaki shorts and olive-green vests, with company-colour *patkas*[2] on their heads. The JCOs and the young officers in white shorts and shirts stood in front of their respective companies. The subedar adjutant (SA) gave the report to the subedar major (SM), who gave it to the adjutant, who in turn gave it to the training officer.

'Companies, *kunj kar* [march off],' ordered Varinder, and under their respective officers, the recruits were off and running to do their assigned training of the day. Everyone would go for a run of 2 to 3 km, followed by some calisthenics and other strengthening exercises. The SM and the SA came forward to where Vikrant and Varinder were standing.

'Sir,' said the SA, 'one of the Agniveers, a recruit, has gone missing overnight.' The recruits were called Agniveers after a new Agnipath scheme introduced by the government a few years earlier. Under this scheme, rather than being enrolled permanently as per the earlier policy, recruits would be enrolled for a term of four years only, with only a small percentage of them being absorbed permanently into the army. There were many pros and cons

---

[2] Cloth headgear

of the scheme that were being hotly debated, but that made little difference to the functioning of the Centre. Their job was to train recruits, period.

'Who is it this time?' asked Vikrant. As the adjutant, it was his job to maintain discipline in the Centre.

'Agniveer Mukhtiar Singh, from number 4 platoon of Kalidhar Company,' replied the SA.

'Mukhtiar Singh? Isn't he the one who failed his drill square test last week?' asked Varinder.

'Yes, it's the same guy. These chaps cannot bear any setback and desert at the first sign of adversity. God knows how we are going to fight a war with such jawans,' said the SM, shrugging theatrically.

'Now, now,' said Varinder, 'don't be so quick to judge. I've seen these boys, and they are sharp and eager to learn. In fact, their standards are far higher than those of our earlier recruits.'

The SM was not convinced. Vikrant told the SA, 'Send a search party to the bus stand and railway station. Perhaps we can nab him there.'

The two JCOs moved off to follow these orders, while the two officers jogged off in the direction of the other fast-receding company columns. PT was compulsory for everyone.

The main office had a designated area where all personnel coming to the Centre whether on first reporting or returning from leave would assemble every morning for a formal interview. Apart from the cohort of that day, the working party of the previous evening had also assembled. The adjutant spoke to each of the returning personnel, inquiring about their well-being. When their turn was over, each individual turned to their right, saluted and marched off. When only the working party was left, the adjutant sent word for Varinder to come down.

'It's strange,' he said, saluting Varinder, 'every one of the recruits from the working party is here, except for Agniveer Mukhtiar. He's the same chap who was reported missing this morning.' The two of them questioned the working party about what they had done the evening of the Mess party and if they had observed anything untoward. Nobody remembered anything. The party had taken place more than two days ago, and forty-eight hours for a recruit is a lifetime. Some of them had helped unload the vehicles, others put up the drop lights. Nobody mentioned anything about the statues of the malis. After trying various ways of eliciting information, Varinder was finally forced to be more direct.

'Did any of you enter the rose garden? Or the Mess building? Do you remember if any of the decorations in the lawn were rearranged?' Even while asking these questions, he had left it open-ended, not wanting to put any thoughts or words into their heads, knowing how perceptive they were, answering as per the mood of their officer. Dismayed at having drawn a blank, he dismissed the working party and told them to rejoin their training schedule.

Subedar Kartar saluted and said, 'It's too bad Mukhtiar has run off. He was showing signs of improvement. In fact, he was practising his drill movements well after dinner for the test slated to take place today. I can't understand why he would have run off after practising so hard.'

* * *

After PT, Renuka got ready a little faster than usual as she wanted to go to the Mess and see the lawns and gardens once again. It was a Thursday and the mazhar on the way to the Mess was again teeming with people offering their prayers. As Renuka was walking past, a young girl wearing a pale blue salwar kameez brushed past and thrust a note in her hand before disappearing into the crowd. Reaching the Mess she unfolded the note. Written in a cryptic but neat hand was the message, 'Urgent, I need to talk to you. I will wait for you at the temple by the *ghat* on the riverside at *aarti* time. Rehmat.' Intrigued, Renuka folded the note and put it in her pocket, wondering whether it had any connection with the case or whether she should tell anyone about it, but she decided against it. *Let me first meet this Rehmat person*, she thought. Renuka was a regular at the evening aarti, so it seemed this person was aware of her movements and that it would be possible to meet there without arousing any suspicion.

The day was spent compiling the statements of the previous day. The statement of the photographer and head mali, Dhani Ram, the observations of the Court regarding the placement of the statues, all of it had to be recorded. Based on the photographic evidence, Anamika's husband, Lieutenant Colonel Mukesh Chaddha was also called.

'What were the two of you fighting about?' asked Varinder, without beating about the bush.

'It was just a normal evening, who says we fought over anything?' Confronted with the photos, Mukesh was forced to admit, 'I was unhappy about her wanting to continue to participate in various pageants. It was fine when she was unmarried, I told her, but now she also had to consider the reputation of the army and the honour of the Regiment.

You tell me, Sir,' he said, looking at Varinder, 'would it be seemly for one of our ladies to be on TV in a bikini, in full view of a million people including our jawans?'

'So, what happened after that?'

'My wife snubbed me and sobbing, went off towards the rose garden. I wanted to follow her, but I was angry, so I turned in the other direction, deciding to go to the washroom to freshen up before confronting her again. Before that, I went to the riverbank to have a smoke.'

'Angry enough to cause her harm?' asked Renuka. 'Angry enough to disfigure her so that she would not be able to participate in any future pageants? And where were you when your wife was attacked?'

Mukesh was visibly hurt at this accusation. 'I would never hurt my wife,' he said. 'I would have reasoned with her, perhaps asked some of the senior ladies to speak to her, but I would never hurt her.' After a pause, he continued, 'I was in the washroom by myself when I heard the screams. Even from that distance, I recognized her voice and rushed to her side. I couldn't possibly have been anywhere near the rose garden. Why don't you check your precious photos and videos? You'll know I'm telling the truth.'

'That's just it,' said Varinder. 'From the time you turned your backs on each other, we have no more photos or videos, neither of Anamika nor of you. You reappear on the scene only when Anamika is being carried to the ladies' room a good fifteen minutes later. Anyway, we will record your statement as per what you have said.'

* * *

After the games period, Renuka changed into her evening dress, ready for her rendezvous with the mysterious Rehmat. She walked down a short flight of stone steps to the temple that was situated on the banks of the river. Being summer, the river had shrunk in size and there were only one or two flowing water channels. Devotees were walking through the sand up to the channel to take a holy dip. From the bank of the river, Renuka could make out that the water didn't seem to be moving fast and it barely came up to waist level. She could hear the pujari commencing the aarti. Glancing around to see if she could spot Rehmat, she went inside and after paying obeisance, sat down along with the other ladies. Immersed in prayer, Renuka did not immediately feel the presence of another body next to her.

'It's me, Rehmat,' whispered a voice in her ear. 'Don't look around. After the aarti is over, continue to sit here. We'll talk then.'

Renuka did as she was told. Rehmat may have looked young, but she had spoken confidently and with authority. After the aarti, they moved to a corner of the temple and looked carefully at each other. Rehmat, thought Renuka, was much like her. Almost the same height and build. The same poise, although her eyes were darting here and there, probably to see that they were alone.

'Who are you? And why do you want to see me? Do you even know me?' asked Renuka.

Rehmat put a hand on Renuka's shoulder to quieten her. 'I'm Rehmat. My mother Zareena is the cook in the commandant's house. In fact, she has been there since the time Rohit's father was the commandant. You might have seen her the day of the cocktails.'

Yes, indeed, the name Zareena rang a bell. Renuka remembered how a person named Zareena had come to the door of the drawing room and how pleased Rohit had been to see her. On the way back after the cocktails, he had spoken about Zareena and her daughter Rehmat. It all made sense now.

'Anyway,' continued Rehmat, 'my mother told me all about you and I have been dying to meet you. You're like a role model to me. But that's not the point. Rohit and I used to play together as children and when I came to know he had returned, I sought him out. Since then, we have been meeting often, usually in the rose garden, away from prying eyes. I know what has happened and that Rohit is in trouble, and I want to help in any way I can.'

This was a lot to digest in one go. So that's where Rohit was disappearing to on most days. While she was going to the temple, he was probably going to the rose garden to meet Rehmat. He had not told anyone about it and had been so discreet that not one of them had come to know of these secret trysts. No wonder Rohit was silent about what he was doing in the rose garden; he did not want to drag Rehmat into an already messy affair. Always worried about the other person's reputation at the cost of his own. That's her Rohit! Or was he Rehmat's? Banishing such thoughts from her head, she asked Rehmat, 'How much do you know about the case?'

'Almost everything. Mrs Menon confides in my mother and since Rohit is involved, my mother fills me in.'

Renuka thought for a while, mulling over the various aspects of the case. 'I'm sure the malis know something,' she said at last. 'But I doubt they will talk to any of us. Perhaps you can find out something? Some gossip in the village square perhaps?'

'Yes, I'll do that. Anything for Rohit.'

The two of them embraced spontaneously and went their separate ways, leaving the temple in different directions.

* * *

The officers were in the Mess later in the evening having dinner. Jeevan was standing in one corner of the dining room, overseeing the stewards as they went around serving the officers. The telephone rang and Jeevan went to answer it. They could hear his muffled voice. 'Yes, Sir. No, Sir. I'll tell them, Sir.'

'That was the adjutant,' said Jeevan, on returning to the room. 'There has been some incident in the garrison. All of you are to return to your rooms.'

'Why? What's happened?' asked one of the dining-in officers.

'Apparently one of our jawans has been found dead, that's all I know. Till such time that the police conduct their preliminary investigations, we are to stay out of the way.'

While walking back to their quarters, they wondered what the incident was all about. A jawan dead? They found the adjutant waiting for them in the lounge.

'Rohit and Renuka, stay here. The rest of you off to your rooms,' he ordered. Once they were alone, he said,

'You remember that as part of the inquiry, we wanted to question the working party?'

When they nodded their heads he continued, 'Well, one of the jawans, Agniveer Mukhtiar, was missing from the morning fall-in. We assumed he had deserted, but he has now been found hanging from a tree in that mango orchard between the Mess and the village. As per initial reports, he has been dead since about midnight yesterday.'

'What's that got to do with us?' asked Rohit.

'We think there's something suspicious. Last evening when we were in the Mess, we had decided to speak to the working party first thing in the morning, and now, of all things, it is a jawan from this party who is dead? It's too much of a coincidence. We are awaiting the post-mortem report, but the police seem to think it is a case of murder.'

'Obviously, Mukhtiar knew something,' deduced Renuka. 'That's why he has been silenced. And this time we know Rohit was nowhere around, so it must be someone else. Someone else who not only attacked Anamika in the rose garden but who has now killed Mukhtiar to cover up his tracks. It's so horrible.'

'Anyway,' said Vikrant, 'I just wanted to tell you that the inquiry is suspended till we resolve this other matter. Just go about your normal duties and Rohit, stay out of trouble.'

Renuka wondered whether to say anything about Rehmat and how she had enlisted her help to do some sleuthing but decided against it. Moreover, she had not discussed it with Rohit, so she stayed silent.

That night, the leopard reappeared. It was loping down the road, running after a figure running away desperately. It was a losing battle, and the leopard came closer and closer and pounced on the flailing, screaming figure, wrestling it to the ground. Rohit looked up from the side of the bed where he had fallen with a thud, bathed in sweat. He checked to see that he was not injured or bleeding from anywhere; the dream had been so real. He could hear Renuka pounding on the door, calling his name. He got up unsteadily to open it and embraced her tightly. Wordlessly, Renuka returned his embrace and led him silently back to his bed, gently shutting the door behind her.

Chapter 6

The Plot Thickens

Walking to the Mess the next morning, Renuka tried to bring up Rehmat in the conversation. The two of them were walking past the mazhar when she casually asked, 'Rohit, have you ever noticed a young girl who often comes to pray here? In salwar kameez and pigtails?'

'Why do you ask? I don't see anyone around.'

'Not right now, silly. I've often seen her as we walk past. It's a wonder you have not noticed this pretty young girl.'

'Why should I be looking left and right when I'm with you?' answered Rohit, deftly sidestepping the question.

Renuka was not one to let go. Once they were seated for breakfast, she nonchalantly said, 'You know, I met Rehmat yesterday.'

Rohit sputtered and nearly choked on his tea. 'What? Where?'

'So, you do know her,' said Renuka, smiling gleefully, pleased at having scored this little victory. 'I met her at the temple yesterday before dinner.' She then recounted the whole sequence of events; from the time she received the note to what they had discussed amongst themselves. 'We have decided to meet again this evening.'

'Where?' asked Rohit, still a little discomfited at this turn of events.

'Where else, in the rose garden, of course,' replied Renuka teasingly, with a wide grin and a twinkle in her eyes.

Later in the day, once the outdoor training was over, the young officers went to the resource centre, where they were being taught the regimental language, Punjabi. An office runner interrupted to say that Rohit and Renuka were to report to the adjutant immediately. 'Now what?' they thought simultaneously, looking at each other. Picking up their books, they marched in quick-time to the main office, which fortunately was not too far away.

'Freshen up,' said Vikrant when he saw their hot and sweaty faces, and added, 'Come to the conference room. We have to brief the commandant.'

When they entered the conference room, they saw that except for the commandant, most of the other senior officers were already there. The deputy commandant, training battalion commander, staff officer training and the adjutant. They took their seats at the bottom of the table and looked around. The room was a longish rectangular one with an oval table that could seat ten to twelve people. On the walls were portraits of past commandants, and Rohit saw the portrait of his father staring down at him.

'That's my father,' he said, giving Renuka a nudge. 'I hope now at least he'll cool down knowing I'm not to blame.'

Renuka looked at him questioningly, but before she could say anything, the adjutant intoned, 'Officers, the commandant.'

'Good afternoon, everyone,' said the commandant once they were seated. 'We have had a very disturbing week. First the assault on a lady in the Mess, and now this suspected foul play. I have been getting regular updates, but I think it would be better if we go through the whole sequence of events from the day of the party and various other pieces of information that have emerged, putting them in some sort of sequence, making some sense out of it and deciding the next course of action.' Looking at the two young officers, he added. 'You should not really be here, but since you were the ones who found out about the photos, I have included you. Everything we discuss is in the strictest confidence, not to be shared with anyone else. Varinder, please proceed.'

'Excuse me, Sir,' interrupted Vikrant, 'before Sir begins his briefing, I would like to update you that the police have received the post-mortem report and it's definitely a case of murder, under BNS, Section 103. Mukhtiar was first drugged, and then strung up on a tree to make it look like suicide.'

'Make a note of that,' said the commandant looking at Varinder, who had moved to the foot of the table, to the large screen display on the wall. He tapped the touchscreen to bring up a Google view of the Mess. 'This will make it easier to understand,' he said. 'I have numbered some of the locations. We were all at the dining-in party for the young officers. The evening was going along fine till we heard the screams from the direction of the rose garden.' Pausing to pick up a laser pointer, he clicked it a couple of times to check that it was working. 'Point 1, is the location of the attack. At that time, Rohit, by his own admission, was at Point 2, which is some distance away. Just before losing consciousness, Anamika had pointed at Rohit and uttered his name, which formed the basis of ordering an inquiry. Anamika, though, has now clarified that she was pointing at Rohit expecting him to say that he had seen something and not accusing him as such. Quite by chance, we came across some unusual photos, thanks to Renuka here, which we have now analysed carefully. One statue is here at Point 3, between the bandstand and the edge of the lawn. The other is here at Point 4, at the edge of the rose garden. We believe someone disguised himself and gatecrashed the party as a mali, moving from one to the other and forming the pair of statues that we are so used to seeing.'

'Could he have disguised himself so perfectly?' asked the deputy. 'And wouldn't we have noticed a human being mimicking a statue?'

'Sir,' replied Varinder, 'it was night-time and the statues were kept strategically in the shadows. Here, let me show you the pictures that aroused Renuka's suspicions.' Tapping the screen, he brought up a set of four photos, two for each of the locations taken from different angles. 'I would like to draw your attention to the top two,' he said. 'See here, in the first, there are two malis, near the bandstand; in the second there is only one. Similarly, in the bottom set of photos, there is only one statue in the first, but two figures in the second. If you see the time stamp, Sir, you will notice that this second pic is just before the attack occurred.'

The figures did look like statues. Looking at the photos, one couldn't make out that it was in fact only one statue and one human.

'What made you suspicious?' asked the commandant, looking at Renuka.

'Well, Sir, apart from there being two statues at two different locations, it was the whites of the eyes that gave me cause to think and that was the giveaway. Could you please zoom in a bit, Sir?' The close-ups clearly showed the difference between the two figures, one with shiny eyes reflecting the glare, and the other not, obviously a statue.

'Can we identify who it is?' asked the adjutant. Maybe the malis can shed some light on who it might be.'

'Unfortunately no,' replied Varinder, 'and the malis are tight-lipped. They are not telling us anything, probably thinking that we will put the blame on one of them.'

Renuka wondered whether she should tell them about Rehmat but decided to wait until there was something useful to report.

'Let's leave the mali thing for the time being and move on. What about this Mukhtiar business?'

'Sir,' replied the adjutant, addressing the commandant, 'I'll address that. To find out who might have moved the statues, we had called the entire working party to question them. However, Agniveer Mukhtiar was missing, and we assumed that he had deserted overnight. Later in the evening, though, a villager reported to the police that he had seen a body, that of a jawan, hanging from a tree in the mango orchard that lies midway between the village and the Mess. The police went to investigate along with our regimental police and that's when we found out that it was Mukhtiar. As I mentioned right at the beginning, it is now confirmed that he was murdered.'

Allowing a moment for everyone to digest this information, Varinder spoke up. 'Sir, there is definitely some connection between the assault, the statues and the murder. Only the previous evening, we had gone on site as part of the inquiry and talked to the malis. When nothing came of it, we decided to question the working party. In fact, Sir, it was one of the malis, Dhani Ram, who made that suggestion. That Mukhtiar, who was part of that party, was murdered before we could question him, is too much of a coincidence.'

'I agree,' said the commandant, '*dal mein kuch kala hai* [there is more to it than meets the eye]. Who was around when you passed the order to call the working party?'

Varinder thought for a moment before replying, 'Well, all the members of the Court to start with, the Mess secretary, who I had called for myself, the Mess staff, Jeevan, our head butler, and maybe a few of the conservancy staff doing their routine cleaning. Surely you don't suspect any of them?'

'Maybe not directly, but we need to keep an open mind. Perhaps one of them spoke to someone who spoke to someone else. You know how news travels. Share our concerns with the police and request them to follow up with the civilian witnesses.' The commandant rose to go, and they all followed suit.

'Just one question though, what was that civilian doing in the forest? Isn't it on army land?'

'That's right, Sir,' said the deputy, 'I had the same doubt too. Apparently, this man's daughter was killed in the same grove more than a decade ago and he goes there every day to place some flowers at the spot where she was found. That's how he came across the body.'

* * *

It was dusk when Renuka and Rohit made their way to the rose garden. While waiting for Rehmat to show up, they took a stroll around the garden.

'This is where I was sitting that day,' said Rohit. 'From here to where the incident occurred, further down this path, is almost fifty metres. It was night-time, the lawns were brightly lit, so this area was in the shadows.'

'I can imagine,' said Renuka. 'Are you sure you did not see or hear anything?'

Rohit tried to recollect those moments. 'I don't remember. I thought I heard Anamika sobbing and maybe she wanted some privacy, and as she was walking in this direction, I got up to rejoin the party.'

'And then what happened?' prodded Renuka.

'Wait. I just remembered something. I think I saw Anamika peering into the bushes to her right and stopping startled. I had just left the garden, when she started screaming, and I turned back and ran full tilt towards her.' While speaking, they had walked in that direction. 'This should be approximately the place where she peered into the bushes. The place where she fell is only a few metres further down.'

Renuka looked into the rose bushes on either side of the path but could not make out anything in the dark. 'We should come here again in the daytime and look for clues. I'm sure there would be some tell-tale signs. Let's go and meet Rehmat, she must have come by now.'

In the darkness around, the fireflies were fluttering about in a merry dance. Absorbed in their investigations, they did not notice the shiny pair of eyes amidst the glow of the fireflies, observing them from a distance. They walked a bit further into the garden, closer to the boundary wall, where Rehmat was indeed waiting for them at one of the benches that dotted the garden. This was Rehmat's and Rohit's usual rendezvous. They had spoken the day before the incident but had not met since. Rohit didn't quite know how to greet her with Renuka around and settled for a quick formal handshake, much to Renuka's amusement. The two girls, however, didn't seem to feel any awkwardness and hugged each other warmly.

'Tell us what you have found out,' said Renuka once they were seated, Rohit sandwiched between the two ladies.

'Most of my information is what I gathered from my mother. I couldn't ask her any direct questions, so this is just what she told me offhandedly while doing her chores.'

'That's perfectly all right,' said Rohit, squeezing her hand. 'I don't want you to be directly involved. There's a murderer around, who knows what he might do next? Just keep your eyes and ears open and stay in the background.'

'Don't worry, nobody notices me. Anyway, my mom says that the whole town knows about the happenings in the garrison, especially the people in the village. That's where the malis and most of the civilian staff come from. They definitely know something. The statues are too heavy for one person to lift, but all of them say they had nothing to do with it. Jeevan, the head butler, had spoken to them while overseeing the preparations, but it was about plucking some flowers for the centrepiece and things like that. Nothing about the statues though. I feel Dhani Ram, the head mali, knows more but he will have to be spoken to privately.'

'What about the murder? Do the villagers know about that?'

'Yes, most certainly. In fact, the murder has overshadowed the Mess thing. The villagers are convinced the overgrown grove and the forest beyond is haunted by evil spirits. They believe a *shaitan,* an evil spirit, lives there who lures people to their doom. Nobody ever ventures there.'

'How did Mukhtiar wind up there then?' asked Rohit. 'Mukhtiar is, was, a new recruit. He would not have heard these tales yet. Did someone lure him there?'

'We think there is some connection between the two incidents,' said Renuka when Rohit paused for breath. She told Rehmat about their meeting in the commandant's office and why they thought the incidents were interconnected. 'The meeting was strictly on a need-to-know basis. So, remember, you did not hear all this from me.'

Rehmat laughingly replied, 'Not to worry, commandant ma'am will tell my mom, and my mom will tell me anyway.'

'We were told about an old man who found the body. What's his story?'

'That would be Badlu Prasad. Many years ago, his daughter-in-law Payal, a young widow, was found dead in the forest, apparently the victim of a leopard attack. She was married to Badlu Prasad's son, Bahadur Prasad, who died during some fighting on the border. He lost both his son and daughter-in-law in a short space of time and became a little mental, deranged, after that, wandering about here and there, mumbling to himself about a tendua. In their memory, he goes to the mango grove where her body was found almost every day.' Looking around at Rohit and Renuka, she added breathlessly, 'Why the villagers feel the forest is haunted is because Mukhtiar was found hanging at the same spot where Payal had been found. Under that very tree in fact.'

'The plot thickens,' said Rohit, mimicking a heavily accented British voice, borrowing a phrase from a play written centuries ago. 'The assault, Mukhtiar's murder and the dead widow are somehow connected. What are we missing?' The three of them sat in companionable silence for a while, each immersed in their own thoughts. So immersed, in fact, that they did not notice a shadow flitting from tree to tree, coming ever closer.

'What do we do next?' inquired Rehmat.

Renuka, who was privy to all the facets of the inquiry, answered. 'We need to dig deeper. Rehmat, you should find out more about Badlu Prasad and his daughter-in-law. There must have been some gossip around that time. Also, the exact day and year too. That will help us dig out the police records.'

'Sir, yes, Sir,' replied Rehmat giving a mock salute.

'In the meanwhile, we will call all the malis one by one to depose individually before the Court. That way, each of them will be able to speak to us in confidence.'

'We can also check from the Records office about Bahadur Prasad, I'm sure there will be a file on him. As a battle casualty, his file would still be current,' added Rohit thoughtfully.

'That seems like a good plan of action. We are a team— RRR—and just like in the movie, we must prevail,' said Renuka, referring to a Telugu film released in 2022, which won an Oscar for its 'Naatu Naatu' song, the accompanying dance moves becoming a rage the world over.

'That's a good one,' said Rohit, adding mischievously, 'But unlike the movie, it is you two girls who will have to do the dancing,' which made both the ladies give him a tight punch in the shoulders. In these high spirits, they decided to break off. Rehmat blew a kiss in the air and disappeared into the darkness, a shadow amongst the shadows. Rohit and Renuka watched her go and turned towards the Mess. In the darkness they did not see the other shadow following the first, the first unaware of the second.

* * *

The other officers were all in the Mess for dinner, so they could not continue their discussion.

'I say,' said Rohit, entering the anteroom, 'isn't that Anamika's husband Lieutenant Colonel Mukesh Chaddha's car parked outside?'

'Yes, he was here with us in the bar having a drink. He must have stepped outside for a moment,' said one officer.

'I think he might have been looking for you,' said another, adding, 'I saw him going out towards the rose garden.'

A steward had just served them their drinks when Mukesh walked in. 'Renuka,' he said without wasting any time on courtesies, 'How dare you go and meet my wife in hospital without my permission? That too when she was still reeling from the shock of the assault. If you go anywhere near her again, I'll file a harassment report against you.'

Shocked into silence, Renuka and the others could only look on dazedly as Mukesh stormed out of the Mess, banging the door so hard that the trophies on the wall rattled in their glass cases. Even Rohit, usually so quick to spring to her defence, was caught off-guard by the sudden verbal attack. This was a side of the officer that they had not seen before, and it made them fear for Anamika's well-being.

Jeevan came in to announce that dinner had been served. 'Your shoes are muddy,' said Major Hemant, the senior-most dining-in officer. He was one of the company commanders, recently posted in, and his wife and children had yet to join him.

Jeevan looked down and made a feeble attempt to clean his shoes, wiping first one and then the other shoe on the back of his trouser legs. 'Sorry, Sir, I didn't notice. It must have happened just now when I went to see off Colonel Chaddha.'

Dinner was a muted affair, the tension of the outburst hanging in the air.

'I wonder why he was so agitated?' ventured Rohit, looking towards Hemant, sitting at the head of the table.

'Oh, he's always been like that. A good officer, but a little hot-tempered and that sometimes goes against him. He once bashed up a jawan during a training exercise. Many feel it was the right thing to do, done on the spur of the moment. But rules are rules, and he had to face the music, got off with a warning if memory serves me right.' Gazing wistfully into the distance he added, 'Being married to such a beautiful woman, I think, makes him feel a bit insecure.'

Renuka and Rohit exchanged a quick glance, as they registered the import of what they had just heard. No wonder he didn't like anyone to go anywhere near his wife.

'Any idea when that was?' asked Rohit.

'Young man, the affairs of seniors should not concern you. Just shut up and eat your dessert.'

After dinner, they all assembled in the lounge of the officers' quarters, which had become a sort of unofficial operations room. A whiteboard in one corner detailed the sequence of events. A felt board that once had had various notices pinned to it had been replaced by blow-ups of the Mess, particularly those that had caught Renuka's attention initially. Naresh passed out mugs of coffee and they all settled down at their favourite spots, Renuka and Rohit on the sofa facing the TV. The incident in the Mess was still fresh in their minds.

'Let's have a look at the party videos again,' said Naresh, 'especially the parts with Chaddha Sir.'

Renuka fished out the pen drive, connected it and pressed the play button. 'Let's watch the whole thing without interruption once. Then we can play it once again, stopping where required. Everyone can make a note of the time stamp so that we can get to that point easily.'

'Good idea,' said Rohit, picking up a clipboard from the centre table in front of him and handing out some sheets of paper. The officers watched the videos in silence, trying to look for any other inconsistencies. At times, a chuckle or groan would escape their lips but for the large part, they watched with intense concentration. When the portion of Rohit and Renuka dancing came on, everyone turned to look at the couple, sitting side by side on the sofa. 'Oh, grow up,' said Renuka exasperatedly. 'Concentrate on the party, not on us.'

Two or three portions of the video stood out.

'See here,' said Sarmah, the techie amongst them, 'there are two statues when the camera starts to pan left to cover the lawn, but when it returns, there is only one at the original position and another at the forward edge where the lawn slopes down to the river.'

They looked more closely at that portion of the clip before fast-forwarding to about ten minutes later. Now they could see two statues near the rose garden. 'What I think happened is, this person inched his way down the slope till he was hidden from view, then moved along the contour to the second place, using the bushes to hide his reappearance.'

'That's a possibility,' said Rohit. 'Whoever it is obviously has a good knowledge of the lay of the land. Any of the malis qualify on that account. We need to look into each of their backgrounds in more detail.'

Next, they looked at the clip of the Chaddhas at various moments in the evening. Initially, the two of them were together, greeting the other officers and ladies and the young officers. As the party progressed, they drifted apart, Anamika sometimes with the ladies, sometimes with the other officers. There was one clip of her talking with the young officers, who were enthralled by her beauty, some of them flirting shamelessly. It was Renuka's turn to chide them, 'Look at you boys, making puppy eyes at Anamika. Are you sure none of you followed her to the garden?' There were howls of protest from all except Rohit, who grinned at their discomfiture.

'C'mon, let's move on. Where is Chaddha Sir during this time?'

After drifting off, Chaddha had gone to the bar and mingled with the other officers, frequently looking around, his eyes searching for his wife. When he heard her tinkling laughter in the company of the young officers, he hurriedly came across and taking hold of her hand, pulled her away, going towards the edge of the lawn. They could be seen arguing, Chaddha even pushing her on one occasion, before they abruptly turned their backs on each other, Anamika going down the pathway towards the rose garden while Chaddha followed the pathway as it disappeared behind the bandstand. As per the time stamps, he was then once again visible only about fifteen minutes later, when Anamika, after being treated in the ladies' room, was being transferred to the ambulance, with Chaddha getting in with her.

'That's a long time to be missing,' commented Naresh. 'But if at all he is the culprit, what possible motive could he have? Maybe we need to speak with Anamika ma'am again?'

'That's another line of action,' commented Rohit. 'Naresh, please note down on the whiteboard all the areas that need to be followed up. Seeing it in writing in front of our eyes will help us focus.'

Naresh rose to do as he had been told and they brainstormed some more. Rohit and Renuka in turn brought them up to speed, without disclosing some of the confidential aspects that the commandant had warned them about.

'There is some link that is eluding us,' said Renuka, glancing at the whiteboard. 'If we could only establish that connection, the pieces of the puzzle will probably fall into place.'

Coffee cups lay scattered about the room, with the occupants sprawled all over the chairs and sofas. A few officers had taken a break to freshen up and were now back in tracksuits or dressing gowns. After no one could think of anything more to add, they decided to follow up on each of the points the following day, dividing the action points amongst themselves.

'Let's work in our buddy pairs,' concluded Rohit. 'That way we'll have each other's backs. No one goes out anywhere alone. Particularly you,' he said, glancing at Renuka. Renuka made a face and stuck out her tongue at him, but even that gesture was so alluring that Rohit hastily averted his gaze. Switching off the lights, they left the room, giving a final look at the whiteboard, with the points scrawled in Naresh's hand.

ACTION POINTS
Talk to malis and do background check.
Whereabouts of Chaddha Sir for crucial fifteen minutes.
Details of Chaddha's bashing incident.
History of girl who was mauled to death.
Police report of the incident.

Speak to girl's father-in-law. Details of his son—KIA.

Speak to Anamika ma'am. With or w/o husband?

Talk to Mukhtiar's buddies. Any strange behaviour?

Girl—Assault—Murder

WHAT IS THE MISSING LINK?

Chapter 7

Connections

Rohit and Renuka were seated in the office of the training officer, Varinder. It had been decided that they would meet there every morning during the tea break to review all matters related to the incidents. Even with the shadow of the inquiry hanging over the Centre, training took precedence. Captain Som Jha came in a bit later and gave them a warm greeting. 'How's it going? All good?' Now that the original Court of Inquiry had been held in abeyance, and since he could proceed on leave as planned, his attitude towards them had changed from antagonistic to neutral. Varinder popped his head in, 'Please be seated, I'll just meet the commandant and come back. Order tea or something in the meanwhile.'

While waiting for him to return, Rohit looked around the room. The windows on one side overlooked a portion of the training area, and from his seat at the table, Varinder could keep an eye on the training, the movements of the squads from one area to the other, and generally get a feel of the tempo of the day. The wall to the rear was almost entirely covered by a horizontal board that had various charts showing training activities, with bar charts vying for space with pie charts and Venn diagrams. Hanging by a cord was a black marker that could be used to update various tables, notably the training state, that is, the number of recruits enrolled, on parade and, if absent, on what account. Under the heading 'Miscellaneous,' somebody had written 'Murder' and the numeral 1 under the absent column. With everyone thus either present or accounted for, the number of Agniveers under training on that day stood at 571. Unlike some offices that gave one an idle feeling, this one pulsated with life and was almost like the heart of the Centre.

Returning to the office, Varinder sat down and adjusted some files on his desk. 'So, what's the latest? Anything more to report?'

Rohit and Renuka looked at each other but stayed quiet, waiting for Captain Jha to take the lead.

'No, Sir, nothing from my side,' he said quite disinterestedly. As far as he was concerned, this whole affair had nothing to do with him. Varinder was quick to sense his mood.

'Right then. Since the Court of Inquiry is temporarily suspended, there is little to gain from having you around.' Buzzing the adjutant on the intercom, he told him, 'Vikrant, Jha can proceed on his leave, but with the proviso of being recalled.' Once Jha had got up, saluted and left, Varinder turned to the young officers. 'Let's get started, shall we? Anything to report?'

Rohit and Renuka moved closer to the edge of their seats.

'Yes, Sir,' they said in unison, making them all break out in smiles. Rohit updated him with all that they had discussed amongst themselves the previous evening, keeping Rehmat out of the picture and not disclosing what they had decided to follow up on.

'We feel we need to look into some aspects in more detail. Perhaps by doing so, we might find a clue to this puzzle,' said Rohit, handing over a sheet of paper with the action points written on it. Varinder went through the list thoughtfully, muttering 'Interesting, interesting' from time to time.

'You have been quite busy, it seems. It's a good plan, though I'm afraid there are some files and documents I cannot permit you to access. I'll follow up on those myself. You both can be present though, when I talk to the malis once again. I'll have them come around at noon when they take their lunch break.'

'Can we at least see Bahadur Prasad's service record?' asked Renuka. 'As also his citation and the AAR, after-action report? There might be something there. And we need to talk to his father too.'

'I suppose so, but I doubt you'll find anything there. It was some counter-terrorist operation somewhere in the North-east, that too, many years ago. I don't see how that can be relevant. As far as talking to his father is concerned, he's a civilian and not under our jurisdiction. But we can try to get him along with the malis.'

'And what about the police report of the leopard attack?' asked Rohit. 'We need to have a look at that too.'

'The two of you are like dogs with a bone,' said Virender in exasperation. 'You do realize I have recruits to train, don't you? Now just bugger off and let me get on with my job.'

* * *

Hastily putting down their cups of tea, they left the office and went across to the other wing of the administrative block which housed the Records office. They explained the requirements to the senior records officer (SRO), who called for one of the records clerks.

'Gaurav, take these two officers and help them find the files they need. But nothing leaves this office without my say-so. You may make notes but no photocopying, as there are legal ramifications.'

Thanking the SRO, they followed Gaurav past numerous rooms, where clerks were hard at work updating the documents of the more than 50,000 or so jawans, serving and retired, who formed the Regiment. Though most of the tasks had been automated, it was nevertheless a laborious and thankless job. Consulting some numbers written on each door, Gaurav finally stopped at one of the rooms and unlocked it.

'This is where the records of the non-effective personnel are kept,' he said. Seeing their perplexed looks, he added, 'That is, those who are no longer in service. However, they or their next of kin still receive a pension, so we have to keep the records safe and updated.' The room was quite large but filled with rows of compactors that made it look cramped and dreary. A small space in between two rows of compactors had a rickety table and two equally rickety looking chairs.

Consulting a slip of paper in his hand that had Bahadur's service number, he went to a row of compactors and turning a large round handle, opened it to the correct place. 'Number 144xxx467,' he muttered as went down the shelves looking for the correct binder. 'Ah, here it is, xx465, 466, 468,' he said, his voice trailing off, going back once again down the line of folders. 'It's strange, xx467 seems to be missing.' He pulled one of the other binders randomly down from the same shelf and gave it a smack, which sent a cloud of dust billowing in the air. 'No one has been down here for ages; I wonder where this particular folder has gone. Wait here while I go tell the SRO. Don't touch anything.'

While waiting for the SRO to come, Renuka rifled through the one folder that had been taken down. It was an exhaustive record of all the details of that soldier, right from the day he joined service, through innumerable postings right up to his retirement, based on which the pension was calculated and disbursed.

'Wow, this is something,' she exclaimed. 'This record is from even before I was born.'

'That's how it is, and it will remain here until he passes away, and until all legal heirs also pass away. Many of these records are close to a hundred years old and have financial effects. That's why the SRO was so concerned about these records. It's strange that this file should be missing.'

The SRO was equally concerned. 'A binder cannot go missing from a locked room,' he said. 'This is a serious matter. I'll probably have to order an inquiry. Who is in charge of this section?'

Gaurav thought for a moment before replying, 'I think its Captain Som Jha, Sir. He was also a member of the Court of Inquiry. He's to proceed on leave later today.'

Before Rohit or Renuka could say anything, the SRO spoke up, 'Seal this room and inform the adjutant. Also send word to Jha that he should come and meet me immediately. He might have to defer his leave till this matter is sorted out.'

They trooped out of the room, Gaurav locking up carefully behind them and pasting a sheet of paper across the door, on which the SRO scrawled his signature. As a temporary seal, this would have to do. While the SRO went off to report to the commandant, Rohit and Renuka returned to the adjutant's office and told him what had happened.

'Bloody strange,' he said accusingly. 'Ever since you lot have come, all manner of weird things are happening. I'll be glad to see the last of you. Anyway, here is Bahadur's after-action report. You can sit in the study room and go through it, but it doesn't leave the building.'

As they rose to go, he thrust a register towards Rohit, 'Sign here as having received the report. And make sure that I record its return.'

Rohit signed and returned the register to Vikrant. 'Bloody strange,' he repeated morosely, shaking his head from side to side. 'Files going missing from locked rooms.'

* * *

The duo retreated to the study room and after ordering some tea and samosas, turned to the folder that had been given to them, a pale pink cardboard file that had seen better days. Pasted on the front cover was a white paper with the heading: 'After-Action Report and Lessons Learnt' and on the next line: 'Ambush on Convoy of 13 SIKH RIFLES, Manipur, 16 November 2006'. Renuka felt a shiver go through her as she opened the file. A real-life after action report. The kind of stuff they had been trained for, not some training exercise with pretend troops and dummy weapons. The report itself was quite cut and dried, written in standard military style—accurate, brief and clear—following a standard format: A short background, details of the incident and actions by various groups or individuals, good points and lessons learnt, names of personnel who had distinguished themselves and a map showing the area where the incident had occurred.

In brief, a two-vehicle mobile patrol was returning to base at about dusk. At a bend in the road, when the vehicles were not visible to each other, an improvised explosive device (IED) had detonated under the lead vehicle, killing or injuring most of its occupants. The second vehicle was also fired upon but the driver, showing presence of mind, sped up and closed the gap between the two trucks. Lance Naik Bahadur, manning the light machine gun (LMG) mounted on the cab of the driver's compartment, returned the fire of the terrorists, firing short bursts into the hillside. As their vehicle screeched to a halt behind the stricken vehicle, lying on its side and engulfed in flames, he jumped down to extricate the wounded. While doing so, he was twice hit by bullets, but unmindful of the danger, he was able to pull two to three men into the safety of the reverse slope. The terrorists, trying to exploit their advantage, came down to the road in an attempt to carry away some arms and ammunition. On seeing this, Bahadur grabbed a weapon of one of the fallen soldiers and charged at them, firing from the hip. Overcome by the ferociousness of a single soldier charging at them, the terrorists turned and fled, but not before a burst of fire caught him full on the chest. Seeing his bravery, the other stunned soldiers regained their wits and established a defensive perimeter till reinforcements arrived. The wounded were given immediate first aid, but by then, darkness had set in and air evacuation was not possible. Sometime in the night, Bahadur breathed his last, still clutching his rifle.

Rohit took a sip of tea before turning to the key pages, the lessons learnt and the personnel involved.

'That's interesting, one of the persons Bahadur rescued was none other than Jeevan, our head butler. That means he must know Badlu Prasad and Payal, and about her unfortunate death.'

Turning a few more pages, Rohit exclaimed in surprise, 'And see here, the officer-in-charge then was none other than our Moti Singh. He was reprimanded for allowing this unscheduled and unprotected movement. No wonder he is a bit disgruntled.'

Renuka, who was studying the map, pointed out. 'See here, the hill from where the ambush was sprung should have been occupied. For some reason, the protective picquets were not present when the ambush was sprung and innocent men lost their lives because of inattentiveness at some level.'

The statistics made for grim reading. Out of the twenty or so men in the patrol, five were killed and twelve injured, with only the odd jawan escaping unscathed.

'We've been looking for connections,' said Rohit. 'And here we have two common factors. However, how it ties up into these events is still unclear. Let's go and share our findings with Varinder Sir.'

* * *

That would have to wait though, as when they reached Varinder's office, they saw the malis lined up outside, waiting for their turn to go in.

'Good, right on time,' said Varinder when he saw them enter. 'I was just going to send word for you.'

'We have a few things to report . . .' began Rohit but trailed off when Varinder gestured him to stop.

'I know of some of the latest developments. We'll discuss those later. Let's finish these interviews first, shall we? We don't want them to spend their entire break outside my office.'

Calling for the runner, he asked him to rearrange the chairs so that there was only one chair in front of the table with the others put by the wall for Rohit and Renuka.

'Here's how we will proceed,' said Varinder. 'I'll call the chaps in one by one and ask if there is anything they might have remembered since. We will spend an equal amount of time with each of them, so that it won't seem that any one of them has blabbed to us. It's very important that they feel safe and believe that what they say remains in confidence.' Calling for the runner, he asked him to send the first mali in and to shut the door behind him.

They interviewed the malis one by one, but not much information was forthcoming. To start with, they felt uncomfortable sitting in the chair placed there for them and would rather squat on the floor, glancing around warily from time to time. The interviews seemed to be a dead end and a waste of time. Varinder was also getting weary and impatient, repeating the same spiel and asking the same questions without eliciting any response.

'We had spoken to you earlier in the Officers' Mess,' he repeated for the seventh or eighth time. 'Would you like to add anything? I assure you whatever you say will remain between us.'

Girdhari Lal, whose turn it was, shifted uneasily on his haunches, looking fixedly between his feet. He glanced up once, gave Varinder a fleeting look and returned to staring at the ground.

'Girdhari *bhaiya*,' interjected Renuka softly, 'please tell us if you know anything about the goings-on in the Centre.

You'll be able to sleep peacefully once you get this weight off your chest, *bhoj halka ho jaega*.'

Girdhari glanced up, surprised to hear her gentle plea. 'Madam, I don't remember for sure, we were all working at various parts of the garden, but I do think I saw Jeevan, Mukhtiar and our senior, Dhani Ram, talking amongst themselves. That's all.'

'Interesting, interesting,' murmured Varinder, signalling for Girdhari to leave. 'I think we need to talk to Dhani Ram once more. Call him again when we have finished with the last chap.'

But Dhani Ram was nowhere to be found. 'He was here only a moment ago. He may have gone to answer the call of nature,' said the runner. 'I'll go check the washrooms.' There was a buzz in the corridor as the malis chattered excitedly amongst themselves and the office runners went to and fro looking for Dhani Ram.

The commandant came out on hearing the ruckus in the lobby.

'I want him found,' he told Varinder. 'Search the grounds and send separate parties to the Officers' Mess and to his house. Find him and bring him here, I don't want any more missing persons or dead bodies.'

Turning back to his office, he added as an afterthought, 'Take a police chap along and check that ruddy mango orchard and surrounding forest while you're at it.'

It took a while for all the necessary orders to be passed and things to return to normal. Once back in his office which the runner had tidied up, rearranging the chairs, Varinder turned to Rohit, 'Now tell me what you were wanting to, earlier in the afternoon.'

So much had happened since the morning that it took a while for Rohit to recollect the exact sequence of events.

'Well, Sir,' said Rohit, clearing his throat, 'you already know about the missing file and Captain Jha's involvement. It's strange, Sir, it's as if someone is reading our minds. Mukhtiar went missing when we wanted to talk to the working party. I told you about our plans only this morning and by the time we went to the Records office, Bahadur's folder containing his service record was missing. Too many coincidences, for my liking.'

'There's one more coincidence, Sir,' chimed in Renuka. 'When we went through the AAR, we noticed that Bahadur and Jeevan were part of the same operation. In fact, it was Bahadur who saved Jeevan's life by extricating him to a safe place. And to top it all, then Captain Moti Singh was the officer-in-charge of that operation, who was reprimanded for operational lapses.'

Varinder looked on thoughtfully. 'I didn't know that. Moti Singh of all people! Surely there is some connection between these events from the past to the events of today. But what?'

They sat silently, each lost in their thoughts, imagining various possibilities.

'We still haven't figured out why Dhani Ram has disappeared,' said Rohit after a while. 'Do you think he felt one of his co-workers might say something? Disappearing like that definitely makes him look guilty.'

'Hmmm, I don't know. Perhaps he knows something, but it's extremely unlikely that he would assault an officer's wife, that too in the Mess. You saw how diffident they were of even sitting in my office chair. But you never know, it could always be a wolf in sheep's clothing.'

'We have two sets of commonalities, Sir,' remarked Renuka. 'Bahadur, Jeevan and Jha who was the custodian of the missing file is the first set; and Mukhtiar, Jeevan and Dhani Ram, our missing mali, is the second set.' Pointing to the boards on the wall, she continued, 'May I make a suggestion, Sir?'

Varinder nodded silently, his mind wandering to the many other pending jobs he had to take care of before he could even think of calling it a day. 'This Venn diagram, Sir, why don't we make one and populate it with what we know? We can have one circle for each of the events: the Manipur ambush, the leopard attack of yesteryears, the assault in the Mess, and the Mukhtiar murder. Maybe that will help us find the missing link.'

'Okay, do that and report back to me tomorrow morning,' said Varinder, glad to get them out of the way. Scarcely acknowledging their salutes, he turned towards the pile of files stacked in his 'IN' tray.

* * *

After dinner, the group assembled in the lounge, now importantly dubbed the 'Operations Room,' which it resembled in a way. While Renuka and Rohit had been away, some more charts had been put up on the notice board, the previous day's 'Action Points' had been typed out in bold font and displayed prominently. There was an air of quiet excitement in the room with everyone eager to share their findings of the day. The aroma of freshly brewed coffee filled the air as everyone settled down in their favourite places, Renuka and Rohit, as usual side by side on the centre sofa.

'Right,' said Rohit, when everyone had settled down. 'Let's all give our reports. We can go in the sequence of our checklist, so that we don't miss out anything. Renuka, you go first.'

Renuka brought everyone up to speed on all that had happened in the main office, especially about the missing file and about Dhani Ram, who was still untraceable. She also gave the details of the AAR and the talk with the malis, leading to the two sets of commonalities.

'I'll write it down on the board so that we can get a clearer picture.' She got up and drew four overlapping circles on the white board as she had suggested to Varinder earlier in the day. In one she wrote, 'Bahadur, Jeevan, Jha' and in the other, 'Mukhtiar, Jeevan, Dhani Ram.' Turning back to look at the others, she asked, 'Does it look all right?' adding with a rueful smile, 'The circles are a bit wonky.'

'Looks okay so far,' said Naresh. 'Why don't you also write "Missing File" and the location "Record Office" in the first circle and similarly, the location, "Officers' Mess", in the second circle? That will give us an idea of the "where?" of the incidents.'

Renuka did as suggested, looking at them for more comments.

'Circle all the missing elements,' suggested Rohit. 'And maybe later, we can colour-code the points. I hope we have different coloured markers. Who's next?'

'I'll go next,' said Sarmah. 'But before I do, perhaps we can add Moti Singh's name to both circles? He was, in a way, present at both places, though years apart. It may or may not be relevant but let's not rule out anything right at the outset.'

After waiting for Renuka to make the entries on the board, he continued, 'It was not easy getting the personal records of Chaddha Sir. All our records are confidential and are kept with the head clerk. Anyway, under the pretext of checking whether all our documents have been received from the Academy, we managed to gain access. We told the head clerk that since all of you were busy with the inquiry, we would check for correctness for every one of us. That gave us an excuse to stay longer, and when the head clerk went out for a while, we sneaked a peek at Chaddha's dossier.'

'That's great,' said Rohit. 'But let's not do anything that will get us into trouble. I'm in enough trouble as it is. I wouldn't want to drag any of you down.'

'Now don't get all righteous on us,' said Sarmah. 'What are course-mates for, after all? Anyway, here's the interesting part. As a young officer, he was quite the ladies' man. In that connection, for entertaining ladies in officers' quarters in contravention to garrison orders . . . blah blah blah . . . he had been awarded a censure. One of the Mess boys had reported him and he gave that poor boy a proper beating, for which he got yet another censure. And guess what, it was right here in the Centre!'

A collective gasp escaped their lips. 'What? Incredible! The coincidences just keep piling up.'

'Where do we put this in our diagram?' asked Renuka. As that stumped them, they decided to take a break, refilling their coffee cups or going for a smoke, some of them going to their rooms to change into more comfortable track pants and T-shirts. Renuka returned as fresh as a daisy, blushing when Rohit gave her an appreciative glance. Before anyone could comment, she took charge, 'When did the Centre incident occur?'

'Sometime in June or July of 2011, probably when they were here on orientation as we are now.' Looking at Rohit and Renuka, Sarmah added, 'Seems young officers always get up to some mischief at the Centre.'

Rohit rolled his eyes and gave him a resigned look. 'Wasn't that about the time of the leopard attack on the girl? I wonder if there's any connection. That's also the time my father was here. I wonder if this leopard thing is somewhere in my subconscious and that's why I get those dreams.'

Renuka consulted her notes, 'We don't have that information now, but assuming there's some connection, I'll put it down here in the "Attack" circle.'

'That takes us to the attack on the girl and talking to her father,' said Naresh, who had been entrusted with following up on this point. 'Not much to report, I'm afraid. The old man keeps wandering around here and there, and is difficult to locate. The police will not talk to us without an official requisition, which the adjutant will have to initiate. The girl who died was Bahadur's widow and Bahadur and Jeevan were together in the ambush. In light of what we have just discussed, we can add Jeevan's name in this circle too.'

They all agreed to it though a bit reluctantly, as there are more than 800 people in a unit and the chances of jawans having served together on more than one occasion at different places were quite high.

'More than a dozen personnel were there in that ambush,' said Rohit. 'It is quite possible that apart from Jeevan, there might be some others serving in the Centre. We can re-check the names from the AAR and see if any of them are posted here now.'

Renuka and Rohit had still not told their group about Rehmat and how she was helping with the investigation. While the others had taken a quick break, they had discussed it amongst themselves and decided to wait for the time being. 'No point involving her directly. We need to keep her safety in mind. The fewer the number of people who know about her the better. She is like our secret weapon.'

'Your secret weapon, you mean,' quipped Renuka, but agreed with his assessment. In fact, Renuka had quite come to like Rehmat for her simple and guileless ways.

'Time to break off. We have to go for PT tomorrow. And one last point, someone seems to know what we are up to. Not us as a group, but the Centre as a whole, as is evident from the missing file and missing person. So, we must neither discuss this with anyone else nor in front of others, especially the Mess staff, buddies, etc.'

On that note, they gave one last look at the unfinished Venn diagram on the whiteboard. Then they shuffled off to their rooms and the lights went off one by one.

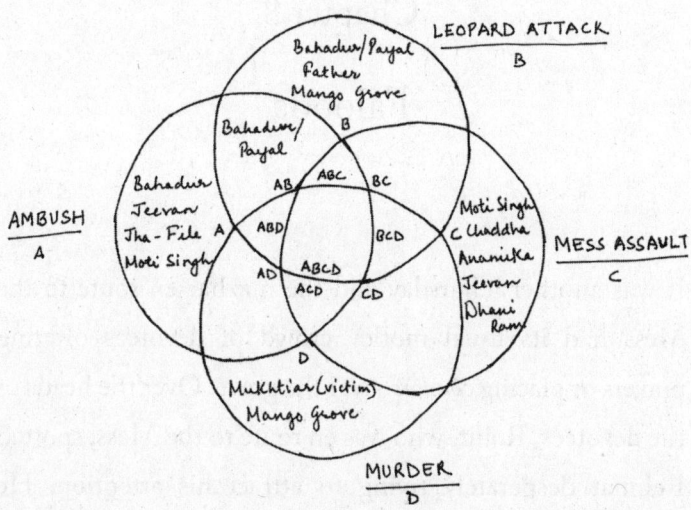

There was silence all around except for the chirping of cicadas and the occasional croak of a frog. From across the river came the plaintive cry of a jackal. All was quiet. But was it? Deftly bypassing the sentry at the gate, a shadow flitted across the lawn and slipped quietly into the lounge. There was a flash of light accompanied by a click, and in less than a moment the shadow was off again, the sentry blissfully unaware of the interloper.

Chapter 8

Falooda

It was another Thursday and the mazhar en route to the Mess had its usual motley crowd of devotees offering prayers or placing *chadors*[3] over the grave. Over the heads of the devotees, Rohit, who was en route to the Mess, spotted Rehmat desperately trying to attract his attention. He nodded in acknowledgement and moved towards the gap in the hedge where they had met scarcely a week earlier. So much had happened since then that it felt like a lifetime. Brushing past her, he whispered, 'Here, take this,' deftly slipping a mobile phone into her hand. 'It's not safe to talk here. I'll call you later.' Rehmat was disappointed since they had not met for a couple of days, but soon regained her optimism. Her very own mobile. It meant Rohit was

---

[3] Decorative cloth sheets

thinking of her. Clasping the phone and nodding, she glanced around and blew a shy kiss towards him. Elated, Rohit walked the remaining distance to the Mess with a spring in his step.

Most of the officers were already at breakfast. 'Good morning, everyone,' greeted Rohit, seating himself in one of the vacant places. 'I don't see Renuka anywhere.'

'I think she is somewhere in the garden,' said Sarmah. 'In fact, I'm waiting for her to come as I have an idea to share.'

A steward came forward to pour them some drinking water and Rohit turned to him and placed his breakfast order. Noticing Jeevan standing discreetly at his usual place towards one end of the room, he asked him, 'All well, Jeevan? What are you feeding us today? Something good, I hope.'

Jeevan, immaculately turned out as usual, answered officiously, 'Yes, Sir. The day's menu is exactly as per the bill of fare displayed on the notice board, as approved by the Mess committee of which you, Sir, are the food member.' Nicely put down, thought Rohit, even as the others guffawed with laughter. It was men like Jeevan, who were the backbone of the Regiment. No nonsense types, straight shooters, but with a wry sense of humour. Rarely did a day pass by without an earthy witticism from one jawan or the other. They might not have been highly educated, but they had an innate common sense and strong notions of honour.

Renuka entered, looking a bit flushed and sweaty. It was still early in the day, but the weather was hot and humid, signalling the imminent onset of the monsoons. Downing a glass of water, she refilled it, even as the steward came forward, and drank that too. 'Bloody hot outside,' she said in answer to their quizzical looks but not saying anything of where she had been. Digging into her breakfast, she turned towards techie Sarmah, who was itching to get his say.

'Listen, after going back to my room last night, I was mulling over the diagram we had made and the entries in it,' said Sarmah. 'I don't know if it struck you, but the opposing sets do not overlap. So, we might miss some crucial connection.'

This was a bit too much to take in so early in the morning, that too before they could even have their breakfast. Understanding their hesitation, he got up and handed around a sheet of paper to everyone, before continuing. 'I've just made a figure of the four intersecting circles we made yesterday, naming them A, B, C, D. If you notice, there is no overlap exclusively between A and C or B and D.' Waiting a moment for it to sink in, he turned the sheet over and showed them a fresh diagram.

'When I realized that, I dug out some of my notes and made this format. It's essentially the same, but now each combination has its own unique cell.'

Naresh grumbled, '*Arre*, I'm a simple infantryman, why are you confusing me with this Venn-shen business. Let's just finish our attachment and get to our units. My unit adjutant is already sending messages wanting to know when we are leaving the Centre and my ETA.'

'I think that's true for all of us,' said Rohit. 'Although I believe we would all be happier if we could settle this matter before leaving, lest it continue to nag us even after we have left.'

There were murmurs of assent which Sarmah took advantage of. 'See here, each of us has this blank format, just fill it out in rough, whatever comes to mind, right or wrong, and give it to me by lunchtime. I'll compile it and have it faired out in time for our evening pow-wow.'

* * *

Renuka and Rohit were seated in the company office, reading their notes and practising for the regimental language exam they had to appear for before leaving the Centre, but their minds were far away.

'What were you doing on the lawns so early in the morning?' asked Rohit.

'I just wanted to go over the "crime scene", so to say, to recreate how our suspect might have moved from one place to the other undetected, considering that we were at least fifty officers and ladies present there,' replied Renuka. 'You know, like in the movies? Everyone just jumped to conclusions, and no one ever thought of actually re-creating the possible sequence of events, or looking for clues.'

Rohit arched an eyebrow. 'And?'

'I sat down on the lawn next to the statue and then inched backwards where the lawn slopes down towards the river. There is a foot track there going down to the river, but also another track going all the way around the Mess. I walked along this path, skirting the lawn and found myself near the rose garden, right next to the other statue. From here, I imagine, our suspect would have had a clear view of Anamika walking towards him after her spat with her husband.'

'And what about where I was sitting? Is that bench visible too?'

'No, not if you're sitting down. Only if both were standing would they be visible to each other.'

'Which means that whoever attacked Anamika did not know someone else was nearby. If only I'd called out,' said Rohit pensively, 'it would have probably staved off the attack.'

'Don't blame yourself,' said Renuka, placing an arm around his shoulders. 'You were just doing the gentlemanly thing by giving her some privacy. Anyway, from there I went towards the gap in the wall.' Seeing Rohit's questioning look, she added, 'You know, the gap through which your girlfriend sneaks in and out of the Mess.'

Rohit gave her a sheepish grin and asked, 'What did you find there?' to change the subject.

'It seems that gap is pretty well used. There is a fairly well-beaten track right from the gap towards the orchard and the village of Muraguri beyond. It also connects to the main road just short of the main gate of the Mess. I think the civilian staff and perhaps even the malis must be using this as a shortcut to come and go. There's a rose bush there too, almost blocking the gap, a rare green rose variety.' Reaching into her pocket, she pulled out a crumpled flower. 'At first, I thought they were leaves, but I googled the image and it turns out it is an extremely rare variety, of a rather temperamental nature. Some even say it isn't a rose at all.'

'You're a walking, talking encyclopedia,' said Rohit. 'But what relevance does it have to our case?'

'Nothing at all,' said Renuka, handing the rose over to Rohit. 'Except that in some countries, it signifies good fortune and new beginnings.'

Now that they had started discussing the case, they put the study material away and instead fished out the new format of the Venn diagram that Sarmah had given them earlier in the day.

'It may look complicated,' explained Rohit, 'but it's actually quite easy to understand. He has even labelled the possible combinations of each cell for us. The centre-most, ABCD will be for those factors that are common to all four events.'

Renuka fished out a pencil and made a couple of entries. 'Need I remind you that I outscored you in maths at the Academy, Mr Know-it-all? No need to show off. Let's make our entries independently and compare the results later.'

They busied themselves, racking their brains to see if they had overlooked anything when the landline phone rang. It was Varinder on the line.

'Good afternoon, Sir. Yes, Sir, she's with me, Sir. Yes, Sir, right away, Sir,' said Rohit putting the phone down and addressing Renuka, 'Varinder wants us in his office. There have been some more developments.'

* * *

The weather had become more oppressive as the day progressed. The air was hot and humid, without even a hint of any breeze. Even the birds, usually seen chirping around in the verdant greenery, had fallen silent, retreating to the sanctuary of the trees. Only the monkeys seemed unaffected, clattering over the rooftops and scampering across the road, terrorizing innocent passersby. By the time Renuka and Rohit reached the main office, barely half a kilometre away, they were drenched in sweat, shirts sticking to their torsos. Reporting their arrival to Varinder, they requested permission to freshen up.

'By all means. Renuka, you can use the washroom attached to my office. Rohit, you can go down to the washroom at the end of the corridor.'

'That's quite all right, Sir, I'll go with Rohit and take turns. I don't want any special treatment.'

Varinder opened his mouth to respond but then thought better of it. *This is one feisty girl*, he reflected. *She's going to be quite a handful for her commanding officer.*

'I've been working on these action points,' he said, when they returned and took their seats, nursing glasses of ice-cold nimbu-pani in their hands. 'Let's start with the girl who was killed in the mango orchard, the victim of a leopard attack. As you know, she was the widow of Bahadur Prasad, who was the hero of the Manipur ambush. I have with me the police report of the incident. I had a deuce of a time tracing it out. Let sleeping dogs lie and all that.' Looking around, he pulled out a file from a tray on the table, marked 'LBW'.

Try as he might, Rohit could not figure out what connection LBW—leg before wicket—could possibly have with the assortment of files in that tray. Before he could contain himself, he blurted, 'Sir, what is this LBW?'

Varinder replied quite smugly, as if he was just waiting for someone to ask that question. 'It stands for Let the Bloody thing Wait,' he said, eliciting weak smiles from his audience. 'This file can't wait though,' he said placing a khaki-coloured, termite-eaten file on the table. 'I have to return it today itself.' Flipping through its meagre pages, he recounted the salient details. 'There was leopard warning issued a few days before the attack and that was the official verdict. However, what Payal—that's the girl's name—might have been doing in the mango grove in the middle of the night, that too all alone, remains a mystery. As Bahadur's widow, she was the legal heir to all of Bahadur's entitlements, running into lakhs of rupees. There was some talk of a fall-out between her and the other family members on Bahadur's side over the death benefits. If she were to pass away before the benefits were disbursed, then those would have to be shared between all legal heirs, as is in this case, which is motive enough for murder. But that's pure conjecture.'

Renuka and Rohit glanced at each other. This was an aspect they had not considered.

'In that case,' asked Rohit, 'why did the police rule out murder? Did they not question Badlu Prasad and any other family members who were likely beneficiaries? Surely, they did due diligence?'

Looking at Rohit, Varinder sighed, 'This is "*dehat*", the backwoods, where the death of a poor girl from an underprivileged family has little meaning. A perfunctory investigation and if a plausible explanation is forthcoming, just close the case. Interestingly enough, Badlu Prasad kept insisting that it wasn't a leopard attack, but it was dismissed as the ravings of a grieving old man.'

It was Renuka's turn to intervene. 'What made them so sure it was a leopard attack?'

Varinder turned over a few pages revealing a sleeve containing some photos of the incident. 'These are the injury marks on the girl's body. See this,' he said, placing one particular photo on the table. 'These injury marks on the back are just what one would expect if an animal were to take a swipe at you. Almost parallel gouges running the length of her back. Her top was shredded to bits as a result, but there were no signs of any sexual assault.' Pausing momentarily, he hesitated, glanced at Renuka and added, 'Though the medical report does say that there were indications of sexual activity in the hours prior to the assault. I think this aspect was kept under wraps and never publicized keeping the *izzat*—the honour—of the Regiment in mind and to safeguard the reputation of a war hero and his wife.'

This was a lot of information to digest in one go. Rohit made some notes on his pad. Renuka scanned through the file, taking a closer look at the photos. They were of poor quality to begin with and over time had deteriorated even further. Pulling out her phone, she took Varinder's permission and clicked shots of each of the photos, including a close-up of the injury marks on the deceased girl's back. Varinder took the file back and returned it to the LBW tray, now pulling out a thick cardboard binder. When Renuka and Rohit looked inquisitively at him, he untied the ribbon that held it in place and explained, 'This is the binder containing Bahadur's service records. When we told Jha he would be able to proceed on leave only after the records were found, he suggested that we look through all the compactors in that room. That's when we found this binder, kept in a different shelf. It could have been an honest mistake, but I have my doubts.'

'Why do you say that, Sir?'

Varinder rapidly turned over the pages, stopping once in a while to look more closely at one entry or the other, while Renuka and Rohit waited patiently for him to speak. 'I get the feeling the file has been tampered with. Some of the pages look a bit newer than the others and even the page numbering is suspect. See here,' he said, pointing to the top right-hand corner of some of the pages, 'the round stamp and colour of ink of the page numbering is slightly different. It looks as if the old pages have been replaced by these newer ones. The initials belong to Jha, so somehow, he is involved in the file going missing and then being conveniently found.'

'Are these changed pages of any importance or relevance to our case?'

'I can't say for sure,' said Varinder with a furrowed brow. 'It deals with the disbursement of his monetary allowances in case of death, disability, etc. Initially, it was in the name of his father, then after marriage, it should have got transferred in the name of his wife as the next of kin, or NOK. After Bahadur's death, she would have got the pension due to him for the rest of her natural life. Unfortunately, she too died, whereupon the pension should have ceased. But it seems that his father, Badlu Prasad, still receives the pension. Either Bahadur did not change his NOK on getting married, or somebody has fudged the records so that the pension keeps coming.'

This was all getting a bit complicated, and the officers asked a few questions to understand the system and the legalities involved in deciding who was the rightful heir of a jawan killed in action. All this information was a bit like the falooda atop a dessert, a jumble of vermicelli noodles that needed to be unravelled.

'Why would anyone do that?' asked Rohit. 'And doesn't it amount to defrauding the government?'

Varinder sighed and said thoughtfully, 'There's two ways of looking at it. If indeed Bahadur had not made any changes, there is no foul play involved. It is not uncommon among our jawans to wait for a few years after their marriage, to see if things are working out, before changing their wills in favour of their wife. If that is not the case, then it's definitely a case of fraud. But then again, maybe someone might have wondered how the father would survive without any fixed income and made this change out of pity or a sense of righteousness.'

There was silence in the room, the only sound being the ticking of the wall clock, reminding them of the passage of time. A steward came in and cleared away the empty cups and plates, asking if they wanted anything else. 'Anyway,' said Varinder, 'I've asked the unit to dig through their records and find out more details. We will know soon enough what is correct. After all, the unit initiated the paperwork, so they will have their copy of all documents. And here is the interesting part—before becoming a records officer, Jha was a clerk posted in the same unit as Bahadur and Jeevan. They might have forged a bond then, all being from the same village. As you found out, Moti Singh was the officer in charge. Between the three of them, they could have fudged the documents. Moti Singh out of a sense of guilt perhaps. Who can say?'

As they sat there thinking, Vikrant, the adjutant, walked in. 'What do I do about Jha?' he asked. 'He's pestering me about his leave.'

Varinder showed him the documents and voiced his suspicions. 'He'll have to wait till this matter is sorted out. Tell him that we are thinking of ordering an inquiry and let's see if that prompts him into saying or doing something out of the ordinary.'

'Right, Sir. About that mali, Dhani Ram, the police have managed to locate him. He'd run off to his uncle's house in the neighbouring village. They are open to bringing him here in case you want to question him.'

'That's good,' exclaimed Varinder. 'Yes, we most certainly would like to question the blighter. I wonder what he has to hide. Let's break off for the time being and meet here again after lunch.'

* * *

Renuka and Rohit had other plans though. Through the civilian room bearer who attended to them in their quarters, they had got in touch with Badlu Prasad, who after much cajoling, had agreed to meet them. When and where to meet remained an issue, as the officers couldn't be seen roaming around in the village and Badlu Prasad couldn't come to the office, if the meeting had to be kept low-key. Finally, it was their bearer himself who suggested that it would be best to meet in the officers' quarters itself. There was a small gate towards the rear, he told them, from where they could enter, and he would take Badlu Prasad to the pantry, where there would be no one else. Hurrying back to their rooms, they wondered how to approach the old man. Would he be too intimidated by their uniforms or by the presence of a woman in the same room? Finally, they decided that Rohit should change into games dress, white shirt and shorts, while Renuka would wear a civil dress, so as not to overawe the old man. They also decided that Rohit should go in first and put Badlu Prasad at ease, and Renuka could enter a bit later.

The two men were already waiting in the pantry by the time Rohit changed and reached there. It was a small, elongated room with a cooking platform on one side that had a gas stove, electric kettle and assorted paraphernalia for making tea and coffee. An old fridge that had seen better days wheezed at one end, while an even more rickety fan, suspended precariously from the low ceiling, made feeble efforts to cool the room. There were two plastic chairs, probably for the staff to rest on and Rohit sat on one of them while the two older men squatted on their haunches on the floor.

'Badlu *ji*,' said Rohit, out of respect for his age, 'thank you so much for coming. You must have heard about the recent happenings in the area. Our jawan was found dead at the same place as your daughter-in-law. We think there might be a connection. Would you be willing to talk about it?'

Badlu Prasad inclined his head and did a namaste in acquiescence. Rohit signalled for Renuka to enter and on seeing her, the old man's eyes welled with tears. He touched her feet reverentially saying, '*Beti, meri beti*' over and over again in a voice choked with emotion. The room bearer hastily filled a glass with water from the kitchen tap, which Badlu gulped down.

'I'll tell you everything. You remind me so much of my daughter. I never believed the story of the leopard attack, but no one would listen to me. Bahadur and Payal had not been married for long, and since he was in a field area, they were together only when he came on leave. It was a happy time for us. After my son died, she was quite grief-stricken and shattered and hardly went out anywhere. Jeevan, the person who works in the Mess, was often around, trying to help us out. After a few years, she became her chirpy old self. I thought she might have found another man, but didn't say anything to her, glad that she had come out of her shell.'

This somewhat gelled with what they had heard earlier in the day. It seemed there was a boyfriend, as yet unidentified, an altogether new piece of the puzzle.

'I don't believe in the leopard attack story either,' he rambled on after drinking some more water, 'The police just wanted to close the case. Although she had been mauled to death, the injuries were not the frenzied attack of a wild animal, but more precise. I've seen mangled bodies before, and there was something different, her face was untouched, beautiful, but she had a terrified look in her eyes.'

He closed his eyes, and a shiver ran through his body. '*Baba*,' said Renuka, 'you've been very brave. Your son would be proud of you.'

Badlu Prasad clasped her hands and touched them to his forehead. '*Beti*, get justice for my daughter. The police never listened to me. I kept telling them to look for a green rose, but they just laughed at me.'

Renuka was instantly alert. 'What green rose? Tell us more about it. We will listen to you.'

'There was a green rose tucked in the bodice of her top and a few were scattered around where she was found, the petals trampled underfoot by the search party. No one gave it a second thought. And you know, the only place where there is a green rose bush is in the Mess. The malis knew of it but kept quiet. She had to have been coming from the Mess when she was attacked.'

This was a sensational input that made Renuka almost jump out of her chair.

'Everyone thinks I'm a senile old man, but I see and hear everything.' Looking at Rohit, he added, 'Rehmat should be careful of where she goes and who she meets.'

'There's just one more thing, Baba, if you don't mind my asking. Do you receive any pension?'

'Yes,' he replied proudly. 'A few months after Payal passed away, I started getting my son's pension. That is how I'm surviving.'

As the two men rose to leave, Renuka gave him a big hug. 'You've been a big help. Come what may, I'll get to the bottom of this mystery.'

* * *

They rushed back to the main office building, after Renuka hastily changed into her games dress.

'Sorry, Sir,' said Rohit, apologizing for both of them. 'We got a bit delayed over lunch.' Varinder nodded for them to sit down. Dhani Ram was already in the room, squatting on his haunches, looking terrified and making small moaning sounds.

'*Maaf kar do*, forgive me,' he said with folded hands. 'Forgive me.'

'Forgive you for what?' said Varinder sternly. 'You're not making sense. Speak up or I'll have you roundly thrashed.'

Dhani Ram gave another plaintive wail. 'I had seen Mukhtiar and Jeevan talking to each other and moving about the lawns. When I heard about Mukhtiar dying, I got scared.'

'That's not reason enough to run away,' persisted Varinder. 'Come clean.'

Seeing Dhani Ram hesitating, Renuka added softly, 'Yes, *Dada*, tell us the truth, we know all about the green rose.'

Startled, Dhani Ram looked fearfully at her, wondering how she knew this. 'Sahib,' he said, looking at Varinder, 'there were pieces of a green rose where madam was attacked in the garden. And that girl who died long ago? There were green roses there too. I promise you, sahib, I had nothing to do with either of the attacks.'

'We'll see about that, Dhani Ram, you have let us and your comrades down.' Calling for the regimental police havildar, he told him, 'Ensure his safe return to the police station and get a signed receipt of his safe return. We don't want any allegations raised against us. Also suggest to them that they should detain him in their lock-up for a couple of days, for his own safety.'

'Interesting, interesting,' said Varinder, as Dhani Ram left the room. 'What's this about a green rose?'

Renuka brought him up to speed. Her own round of the lawns and how she had chanced upon the rare green rose bush tucked away near the boundary wall.

'There's only one such bush in the station, and that's in our Mess. Each colour has its own significance, and a green rose symbolizes rebirth, beginnings, growth and good fortune in relationships. It signifies the hope and joy that comes with starting a new relationship.'

'Where did you learn all that?' asked Varinder appreciatively.

'I googled it,' replied Renuka sheepishly. 'But the point is that it must have been given to the ladies by the same person as very few would know the significance of this colour. We need to check who all were in the garrison on these two occasions.'

'That's an impossible ask,' said Rohit. 'The events are more than a decade apart. The recent event, yes, we would have a record of that. But of that period fifteen years ago? Impossible!'

'There's a shortcut for that,' said Renuka. 'We'll just see who all were in the garrison last week, especially at the party and then check where they were on that day fifteen years ago. Obviously, it cannot be any of us young officers.'

Turning to Varinder, she asked him guilelessly, 'Where were you, Sir, fifteen years ago?'

'Thankfully nowhere near the Centre. In the summer of 2011, I was with my battalion on a United Nations mission. So unfortunately, Renuka, you'll have to strike me off your list of suspects. But I know what you mean. There would probably only be a handful of officers who have been to Centre twice.'

'What about Chaddha Sir?' asked Rohit on the spur of the moment. 'Why don't we start with him?'

'That's easy,' said Varinder. 'I have the record of service of all officers currently on the strength of the Centre on my desktop.' Swivelling his chair, he clicked his mouse a few times, pulling up the required file. 'Hmmm. That's a lucky shot. Chaddha was commissioned in June 2011, and though not on the record, he would have been here on attachment, just as you are now.' He scrolled down the file and exclaimed. 'Well, I never knew. During this same period, he had also been awarded a reprimand for entertaining women in his quarters, as well as a censure for bashing up one of the Mess boys. Seems to be quite a character.'

'Perhaps we should have a word with him?' asked Rohit. 'He should be somewhere around as the games period is going on.'

Varinder glanced thoughtfully out of his window at the training area. 'It's a good idea,' he said. 'But I think we should find out more before confronting him. The evidence against him is circumstantial at best. We don't want to give away our hand.'

* * *

Dusk was setting in by the time they left the office, Varinder looking wistfully at the clock and the pile of files awaiting his attention. Rohit had during the day texted Rehmat to meet them at the temple by the riverside. They would have been quite conspicuous in their white games dress, so they hurried to their rooms and changed to civvies. They walked side by side towards the temple, greeting other officers and ladies out for an evening walk who returned their greetings with broad smiles and approving looks. Going down the slope towards the ghat, Rohit offered Renuka his arm, and they walked hand-in-hand the rest of the way, reaching just in time for the aarti. After the evening prayers, they found a quiet spot and waited for Rehmat, Rohit checking his phone every now and then.

'As-Salaam-Alaikum,' said a quiet voice from behind them, which made them jump out of their skins.

'Rehmat, you scared the hell out of us,' exclaimed Renuka. 'Please don't do that again.'

Rehmat chuckled gleefully, quite pleased that she had succeeded in scaring two brave army officers.

'Come, sit down,' said Rohit, taking her hand. 'We don't have much time. Plus, I don't want you roaming around after dark.'

Rehmat sat down between them and thought for a moment before speaking in a precise manner. 'As usual, what I know is what my mom has told me. The villagers are quite intrigued by the renewed interest in Payal's leopard attack case. There is an elderly lady attendant, an ayah who attends to female patients in the military hospital. She was by Anamika's side throughout her stay in the hospital, often helping to change her dressing and making sure she took her medicines as scheduled.'

'Nothing unusual about that,' said Rohit. 'An ayah is always present whenever a female patient is being treated.'

'That's true, however, the ayah says that there is a lot of similarity between the injury marks on Anamika's back and those of Payal's. This has spooked the villagers no end.'

Renuka pulled out her phone and scrolled to the photos she had taken earlier. 'Do you mean something like this?' she asked, showing Rehmat the photos. Rehmat looked at the photos, but shook her head. 'I can't say. There's nothing for me to compare—no reference point. The ayah only said that the injury marks were quite similar. She's the one to ask. Do we have any pics of Anamika's injuries?'

'The doctor did testify at the inquiry, but the focus then was more on me,' said Rohit. 'I don't think we paid much attention to the exact nature of the injuries, except that they were severe.' Patting Rehmat's hand, he added, 'Well done, this is something to follow up on. Anything else? What about the father?'

'You mean Bahadur's father? Poor man, he keeps wandering about here and there, telling anyone who is willing to listen about his son and daughter-in-law and what a wonderful couple they were. Everyone has heard his stories so many times that they avoid him like the plague. Openly no one says anything, not wishing to speak ill of the dead, but some of the villagers say she was probably having an affair with some *bara sahib*, some senior officer.'

'What a scandalous accusation to make,' said Rohit irritably. 'That way, people will even say that you and I are having an affair. People have nothing better to do than gossip.'

'Why are you getting angry with me? I'm just telling you what my mother told me. Moreover, we are childhood friends, so our relationship is altogether different.'

'Sorry, Rehmat,' said Rohit putting an arm around her shoulders and giving her a hug. 'I was thinking about you. We'll all be leaving soon, and you will be left behind all alone.'

Rehmat rested her head on his shoulder and smiling brightly, brandishing her mobile, replied, 'But I won't be alone, will I?' But the catch in her voice and tears in her eyes belied her bright smile.

Chapter 9

When Venn

It was a long walk back to the Mess in the dark. An owl hooted somewhere in the darkness, and they could hear the flutter of birds nesting in the trees that lined the road. The sky was overcast without a single star to be seen. Flashes of lightning in the distance and a cool breeze hinted at the possibility of rain. Not wanting to be caught out in the open, they quickened their step. Rohit took out his mobile and switched on the torch to light up the way. Good thing too, for they had hardly walked a few hundred yards or so when Rohit halted abruptly, holding out his arm to stop Renuka, focusing the torch on something shiny just a few yards ahead. Renuka gasped and held on to his arm when she saw that it was a snake slithering across the road.

'Stay still,' said Rohit. 'There's nothing to worry about, this is quite common around here and that's why we are always advised to wear shoes rather than slippers and to always carry a torch.'

'What do we do now?' asked Renuka, watching the snake slither unhurriedly across the road.

They waited a while for the snake to disappear into the undergrowth and then warily walked past, continuously shining the torch at the place they had seen the snake disappear. Renuka activated the torch on her mobile too, and continuously scanning for any more surprises, they soon reached the safety of the Mess.

The other officers were already at the dinner table, and they joined them and quickly served themselves. There was hardly any talk at the table; everyone seemed to be engrossed in their own thoughts. When the stewards came around to ask if they wanted coffee, they all shook their heads and headed out, eager to get back to their quarters for the post-prandial discussions in the self-styled operations room. When Renuka told them about their encounter with the snake on their way to the Mess, everyone took out their mobiles and shone their torches all around, and it looked as if a ball of light was floating along the ground. Reaching the officers' quarters, they decided to change first into more comfortable clothes, anticipating a long night ahead. Returning to the lounge they took their usual places, mugs of coffee in hand, Renuka tucking her feet under her on the sofa.

'I have here the new diagram I gave you at breakfast,' began Sarmah without any preamble. 'I have entered the points as best I could, from your individual records. It'll take too long to draw, so I'll flash it on the screen.' While they had gone to change, Sarmah had synced up his laptop to the TV and now the Venn diagram popped up on the screen. 'It will be easier to make changes too, and we can even colour code the entries.'

They studied the diagram in silence for a while, trying to understand it and to check whether their points had been considered and placed in the correct cell.

'It seems okay to me,' said Naresh and everyone else murmured their assent. 'Anything more to add?'

'There are two or three things that have come up,' said Renuka. 'We don't know how relevant they are and where they fit in.'

'Just tell us,' said Sarmah, hands on the keyboard. 'I'll feed it in, and we can decide where it fits later.'

Renuka did just that, filling them in on the developments of the day, Jha and the missing file; and its financial connotations, which were still unexplained. Their talk with Dhani Ram the mali, and some connection between Jeevan and Mukhtiar. The mystery of the green rose and how, of all things, Chaddha was present in the Centre on both occasions, an aspect they had overlooked. She showed them the pics of the injury marks from the leopard attack and how they somewhat matched the marks on Anamika's back.

'WhatsApp these images to me,' said Sarmah, 'and I'll upload it to my laptop. It'll be easier to compare once we get photos of Anamika's injuries.'

'That's the problem,' said Renuka. 'Her medical documents are confidential. It's not as if we can just walk in and ask for them. Maybe tomorrow I can go around and have a word with that ayah.'

'What you say is true, but the inquiry against me is only suspended and not closed. Maybe we can call the doctor, Prabhu, once again and see if he has any photos of the injuries.'

'It's quite unlikely that they would have taken a pic of a woman's bare back but no harm in asking. If nothing else, we can show him the leopard attack pics and see what he has to say.'

Sarmah started keying in the various inputs he had received.

'While Sarmah is updating the diagram,' said Rohit, 'why don't we have a look at the party videos again? Each of us should pick one person and let's see if we can track their movement, presence and absence for the entire evening. I'm particularly interested in Chaddha and Jha, both of whom figure prominently in the narrative.' Plugging in the pen drive, he started the video.

'There we are,' said Naresh, 'looking so smart and handsome. That's the commandant and deputy commandant and their lady wives receiving us. Surely there's no reason to keep a tab on them?'

'No, of course not, just the dramatis personae appearing in our narrative,' said Rohit.

'Is that Jeevan, standing behind the commandant?'

'Must be,' said Rohit. 'As you know, he's always just a few paces behind the senior-most officer present, in this case the commandant, ready to take on any request.'

'This is where Chaddha disappears after their spat,' said Renuka. 'And he reappears only about fifteen minutes later, that too near the ambulance. That's enough time to do the deed in the rose garden, sneak out through the gap in the wall and re-enter the Mess from the front entrance.'

'Wouldn't the sentry at the gate notice?' asked Rohit.

'Well, we haven't explored that line yet, but I doubt any sentry would recollect anything as routine as an officer entering the Mess. Moreover, with the hullabaloo on the lawns, just like us, the sentry's attention too would have got diverted,' said Renuka.

'There's Jha,' pointed out Chaudhari, the brainy one of the course. 'He seems harmless enough, but can you go to that part where Chaddha Sir and Anamika ma'am are talking? Yes, stop there. Can you zoom in please? What do you think she has in her hand, slightly hidden by her purse? Does it look like a green rose to you?'

They looked more carefully at the grainy blow-up but couldn't be sure.

'Hey techie,' said Rohit, addressing Sarmah, 'can you do something about this pic to improve its resolution?'

'Sure thing, boss,' said Sarmah, keen to demonstrate his wizardry. 'Just wait a bit, and voila!' Sure enough, in the touched-up version, a green rose was clearly visible.

'I wonder how we missed that,' mused Rohit.

'We didn't know the significance of this earlier,' said Renuka. 'That's why it didn't strike us. But it clearly shows some connection between the leopard attack and the Mess assault. Chaddha seems to be a common factor.' Looking at Rohit she added, 'We must tell Varinder. This is enough to call him in for questioning.' Turning to Sarmah, she asked, 'How's that diagram coming along?'

'Just a second,' he replied. 'Let me close this photo app, and put the Venn diagram up,' and with a few clicks of the mouse, it was up on the screen.

AMBUSH		LEOPARD ATTACK		MESS ASSAULT
Bahadur Jeevan Jha (file) Moti **A**	**AB**	Payal Mango Grove Injury Marks Green Rose **B**		
Jeevan Moti **AC**	**ABC**	Injury Marks **BC**	Chaddha Moti Jha Malis Mukhtiar Jeevan Injury Marks **C**	
Mukhtiar **ACD**	**ABCD**	**BCD**	**CD**	**D**
Mukhtiar **AD**	**ABD**	Mango Grove Injury Marks **BD**	Mukhtiar Mango Grove	MURDER

* * *

Rohit and Renuka accosted Varinder early next morning at the PT parade itself. They excitedly shared their findings and what needed to be done.

'Hold your horses,' he responded. 'First go and do your PT with the troops. Remember, we are here for a purpose and soldiering is our mission. Don't ever forget that or get diverted to extraneous matters, however important they might seem at the time.'

They had to sprint to catch up with the company squads, which by then had gone a fair distance. Renuka took off as was her wont, trying to reach the head of the column. Rohit caught up with the last squad where one of the jawans was having trouble keeping up with the pace, limping slightly, with one hand clutching his waist.

'Something the matter, Amardeep?' Rohit asked. 'Is your leg paining or have you got a catch?'

'Actually, sahib, I've been wanting to speak to you. It's about Mukhtiar.'

'Yes, what about him?'

'I never believed the suicide story. I am, was, his buddy and there were no secrets between us. He had joined the *fauj* after many trials and tribulations, and his family was dependent on him. He was always doing his best, intent on becoming permanent. Something or someone must have misled him. He had two mobile phones, one of which was found on his body. The second he would hide in his kitbag. When we heard the news of his going missing, I fished out the phone to see if I could locate him, but it is locked.'

'So where is the phone now?'

Amardeep pulled a phone out of the pocket of his shorts and thrust it into Rohit's hands. 'I'm sure you'll find something there.' Suddenly sprinting away, he tossed over his shoulder, 'And by the way, there's nothing wrong with my leg,' leaving Rohit behind, jaw agape, in the middle of the road.

Rohit jogged along, his mind abuzz. Every day seemed to bring a new twist in the tale. He caught up with the rest of the group as they returned to the main grounds. As soon as the whistle blew to signify the end of the PT parade, he sought Varinder out and handed over the mobile.

'I'm sure we will be able to see who Mukhtiar was in touch with and find out why he went to the orchard in the middle of the night. I tried to open it, but it's password-protected.'

'Not to worry, we have a detachment from the Signals, who look after our army communications. I'm sure there will be someone who can help. Worst case, we'll take the help of the local police. Well done, young man, now trot along and meet me with Renuka in my office later today, around 1030 hours or so. I should be back from my morning rounds of the training area by then.'

Rohit told Renuka of the latest developments and about their 1030 hours appointment. 'That's great, but why did Amardeep come to you and not go directly to his company commander or adjutant?'

'Well, he was a bit scared since he had not told anyone about it earlier. He had taken the mobile in good faith, but then he got scared when Mukhtiar was found dead.'

'So why come out now? He could have just thrown it away.'

'Mukhtiar was his buddy, and he couldn't just let it go. So he spoke to his father, Subedar Lal Singh, who is in my unit. Subedar Lal Singh has known me since I was a kid. In fact, he's the one who taught me driving. When he learnt that I was here, he told his son to come to me and that I could be trusted.' Turning towards Renuka, he gave her a playful punch in the shoulder and added, 'There are advantages of being a third-generation officer after all,' getting a sharp jab in return.

They met Varinder at the appointed time and gave him an update, showing him the blow-up of the photo with the green rose in it. Sarmah had also printed out a copy of the updated Venn diagram which they handed over and explained its various entries. They also mentioned the timings in the video showing all those who were at various places at different times.

'Sir, everything points to Chaddha, his behaviour has been suspect right from the start. He even threatened Renuka in the Mess the other night.'

On seeing Varinder's inquiring look, Rohit clarified as to how Chaddha had come looking for her and threatened her with dire consequences, if she ever spoke to Anamika again.

'Ah yes, I heard about that. Renuka, you were out of line going to the military hospital like that. I feel Mukesh, like any concerned husband, is just protecting his wife, nothing more.'

After studying the mass of papers on his desk, he gathered them all up and stacked them in a file. 'Time to brief the commandant. Wait here and I'll send word if you are required.'

Rohit stood looking out of the window. So much had changed, yet so much was still the same. What had earlier been barren patches of land were now lush with trees, ashoka, gulmohar and eucalyptus, either lining the pathways or providing much-needed shade to the recruits. The short range was just where it was, though the firing point now had a roof over it, so that firing could continue even during a light rainfall. Through the open window, the sound of firing could be clearly heard, and a trained ear could make out how the firers were faring. He was about to comment about it to Renuka when his reverie was interrupted by the commandant's runner, who saluted and said, deferentially, '*Commandant Sahib ne aap donon ko yaad kiya hai*,' which translated literally means 'the commandant is remembering you' but which actually means 'get your butts in here'.

Brigadier Ashok Menon was at his desk looking at the papers and photos that Varinder had given him. Without looking up, he waved a hand for them to sit down. Running a hand through his hair, he looked up and there was a twinkle in his eyes. 'You have been as busy as bees. I only hope you work as hard when you reach your units. I never even knew there was something called a green rose. And who is the bright spark who designed this diagram?' Laughing, he added, 'I haven't seen one of these since my student days. I never thought it had any practical use. So, youngsters, what is your hypothesis?'

Rohit and Renuka looked silently towards Varinder, who was about to speak, but the commandant gestured for him to remain silent.

'Yes, Rohit, what do you have to say?'

'Sir, we have just put together all the pieces, but I'm not sure we should be commenting about a senior officer.'

The commandant gave a deep, philosophical sigh, 'There will be many times in your life, son, when you will be faced with such a moral dilemma.' Pointing to the wall, he said, 'Do you see that quote of Guru Nanak there? "The only thing necessary for the triumph of evil is for good men to do nothing." Just remember that.'

'Sir, as you yourself mentioned, not everyone knows about this rare variety of rose, and the green colour signifies among other things, a new beginning. I think Chaddha Sir knew Payal, Bahadur's wife. I cannot say anything about the depth of their relationship, but it's quite possible that they were romantically involved. Maybe it was a case of unrequited love.' Rohit paused, looking at Renuka, who nodded in support, encouraging him to continue. 'Chaddha and Anamika ma'am were having some marital issues, probably over her wanting to continue participating in beauty pageants. Giving her a green rose was once again like asking her to forget her past and move on. And . . .'

Seeing Rohit hesitate, Renuka chipped in, 'But whether he is involved in any acts of violence, we cannot say for sure. He was upset though, that I had spoken directly to Anamika, and we also know that he has a quick temper and is prone to violence.'

This time it was Varinder who broke the silence, 'I think, Sir, that it would be best if we called Chaddha and asked him face-to-face what he has to say about it. Let us not jump to conclusions.'

'Right, do that. Brief the deputy commandant and let him call Chaddha for a chat. Let me know the outcome. As for the two of you, get back to the training area. Enough of shamming.'

Renuka and Rohit jumped to their feet. 'Yes, Sir! Right away, Sir,' they said in unison.

'Just one question, Sir, before we leave,' said Rohit. 'While reviewing the video of the party, we saw that you often turned your head from side to side.'

Mimicking the motion, Renuka asked, 'I hope everything is all right, Sir? Some pain in the neck?'

'You're the pain in the neck,' joked the commandant. 'Everything is absolutely fine. Thank you for asking. I was probably looking for Jeevan to ask for a drink or something, he's usually always underfoot.'

* * *

Mukesh was at the rifle ranges supervising the firing practice of the Agniveers. He had to admit that the standards were higher than what he remembered of his under-training days. He had fired as part of the first detail of eight firers, as much to keep himself current as to demonstrate his prowess. At least two of the Agniveers, with barely four months of training, had scores that were close to his, 26/30 to his 29/30. His attention was diverted by the sound of the dispatch rider (DR) bouncing along the dusty track that led to the ranges. 'Now what?' he thought to himself. The sight of the DR, at any time of the day or night, was never good news. His fears were confirmed when the message that the DR handed over was to report forthwith to the deputy commandant. Telling the DR to return, Mukesh checked to see the progress of the firing. Only one more detail was left for the day, so he decided to go ahead with the last round, rather than having to repeat the whole schedule on another day. Once the last detail had fired, he checked and recorded their scores and signed off on the firing point register. Each of these individual scores had great value as it would be a factor in determining the final merit list. Asking the JCO in-charge to take over, he turned to leave, firing up his Harley-Davidson Sportster S. With an engine capacity of 1200+ cc and 120+ bhp, it was a mean machine. He couldn't really afford it, but he had bought it to impress Anamika, and it was worth every rupee. When they were on the road, going full throttle, Anamika holding him tightly about the waist, nothing else mattered. Thinking about Anamika brought him back to planet earth. He had a fair idea as to why the deputy commandant had called him. The only question was—how much did he know? And how much information should he volunteer? The going was good, he had a promising career, a beautiful wife; why rake up the past? Better to let sleeping dogs lie. Moreover, such matters were between a man and his wife, in which others should not interfere.

Parking his bike, he made his way to Colonel Ravindran's office. The deputy commandant waved him in and pointed to the sofa set on the other side of the room. That's strange, thought Mukesh, one normally met senior officers formally while sitting on opposite sides of the office table, and not in this informal seating. In fact, he couldn't remember sitting here at all. Ravindran picked up a file from his desk and joined him.

'Everything all right?' he asked. 'How's Anamika? I believe she has been discharged from the hospital?'

'Yes, Sir, all is well. Anamika is at home and recuperating. Anything the matter, Sir?'

'Well, it's about you and Anamika that I wanted to speak to you. I believe there are some differences?'

'Everything is absolutely all right, Sir. She's just had a traumatic experience, that's all. It's for us to handle, and there's no reason for anyone to be poking their nose into our private lives. That crazy girl is giving wrong ideas to everyone.'

'Ah, that's true,' said Ravindran. 'But if some argument or affray occurs in a public space, then it does not remain a private matter. You did fight with your wife during the party, didn't you?'

Ravindran turned on the laptop that lay on the centre table and tapped a few keys to bring up the video of the party. He pressed play and turned the screen towards Mukesh. They watched the reel silently, Mukesh seething with anger. *That photographer needs to be dealt with*, he thought, *just wait till I get out of here.* When the clip played out, Ravindran looked expectantly at Mukesh.

'There's nothing to tell. We were arguing and at one point, I pushed her, and she stumbled because of those high heels. Is it my fault that her heels got stuck in the paving? I had told her to dress appropriately, but no, she has to behave like Miss India all the time.'

'Yes, we know about the argument. It seems she did not agree to stop participating in beauty pageants. So how did that make you feel? Angry enough to lash out at her?'

Mukesh was stunned by this development. Did they seriously believe that he had assaulted his own wife?

'That's crazy, Sir. How could you even say that? I admit I was angry. I walked around for a while, going to the edge of the lawn overlooking the river and smoked a cigarette, before going to the washroom. The sight of the river flowing tranquilly had soothed my temper. I was on the point of returning when the quiet was shattered by Anamika's screams.'

'Okay, I believe you. But tell me, what's this in Anamika's hand?'

'I can't see anything apart from her purse. Why?'

'Look closely,' said Ravindran, blowing up the photo. 'Slightly covered by the purse—do you see that greenish looking thing?'

Mukesh was a bit taken aback but decided to brazen it out. 'I'm not sure what it could be, perhaps something she picked up from the garden.'

'You know, Mukesh, we are having this informal chat. We can ask Anamika and if she says something different, perhaps that it was something you had given her, then it will look bad for you. Now's your chance to come clean.'

The wily old fox, thought Mukesh, *he knew about the green rose all along. Wonder how much more he knows.*

'Ah that, Sir, is a rose that grows in the garden. I thought it was pretty so I picked one to give to my wife.' Looking not the least bit contrite, he added, 'That's allowed, isn't it? To give flowers to your wife?'

Colonel Ravindran let that remark pass. *Let him have his small victories.*

'Will that be all, Sir?'

'Not quite, there is another matter that needs to be cleared up. Do you remember when you were here on attachment, a young girl had been found dead in the mango orchard, possibly the victim of a leopard attack?'

Seeing Mukesh hesitate, he added, 'The Centre had been placed on high alert and a special leopard watch constituted? All the officers were part of the search party?'

'Yes Sir, I remember,' admitted Mukesh, wondering why such an old matter was being raked up now. 'We left soon after that on termination of our attachment. Why do you ask, Sir?'

'Since you left soon after, you may not have come to know, but in the evidence that was collected was a green rose, tucked into the bodice of her dress.' Pausing for a while and giving Mukesh a searching look, he added, 'It's quite strange that a rare rose, which is only found in our Officers' Mess, was found at both sites.'

'How should I know? Anyone could have given Payal the rose, it's not as if the rose bush is under lock and key.'

'Was that anyone you by any chance? Even after all these years, you remember the girl's name.'

The best form of defence is offence, thought Mukesh. 'Even if it was me, what difference does it make? We are no closer to finding out what happened to my wife. That's what we should be concentrating on.'

Without waiting for permission, Mukesh rose to go. The deputy watched him for a moment wondering whether to ask him to sit down. Better to let him go. 'We're doing our best. Anyway, we not only think that the cases are connected but also believe that Payal might have been murdered, and it was made to look like a leopard attack, just as Mukhtiar was murdered and it was made to look like suicide. So I'd watch my step if I were you.'

* * *

Rohit's phone buzzed twice and stopped. It was a missed call from Rehmat. He quickly checked for any messages but there were none. It was quite unlike Rehmat to call, especially since she knew that they couldn't attend to phone calls while on parade. Fortunately, it was a short break between two classes, so excusing himself, Rohit went to the side and returned the call.

'Hey! What's up? All fine?' he asked when Rehmat answered the phone.

'Yes, where are you now? Can you come and meet me?'

'Why, what's the matter? I've got a class coming up but will get free in about half an hour.'

'Okay, then come straight to the military hospital. That ayah I was telling you about? She has something to tell us but will only talk to you.'

'All right, where should we come?'

'Tell me when you are done, and I'll text you the location.'

Before Rohit could reply, she had cut the call, leaving him so intrigued that he could not concentrate, eagerly waiting for the whistle that would signal the end of the day's training.

Rohit and Renuka hurried towards the military hospital, wondering what news Rehmat wanted to share. Rehmat had messaged that they should come to the cafeteria, so asking for directions, they went there and found an empty table in a corner. The cafeteria was bustling with activity, patients accompanied by attendants or relatives, and off-duty staff mingling with harried servers scurrying around. They were the only officers there, but no one gave them a second glance. The aroma of idli-dosas and channa-bhatura made their mouths water but not wanting to get distracted, they just ordered some filter coffee, which was plonked unceremoniously on the table by a sweaty waiter, coffee dripping down the sides of the stainless-steel tumblers. Rehmat had brought the ladies ward ayah along, and after taking a few sips of coffee, Rehmat turned to her.

'Jagvati *Dadi*,' she said respectfully, 'will you please tell us why you wanted to meet us so urgently?'

Renuka nodded, 'Yes please, Dadi. I remember seeing you in the women's ward. Does this have something to do with Anamika?'

Jagvati adjusted the *pallu* of her sari and glanced around. 'As you know, madam, I was attending to Anamika ji during her hospitalization. I was there throughout, from the time she was first brought in, and saw her injuries first-hand. Something about her injuries troubled me, so one day, without anybody's knowledge, I took photos of the gouges on Anamika's back.'

Jagvati paused, waiting to see their reaction and expecting some admonishment. Encouraged by their silence, she brought out her phone. With a few practised touches, she opened the photo gallery and selected a photo, turning the phone around for them to see. Even though the wounds had healed somewhat, it was still a terrifying sight. Four almost parallel angry red welts running down the length of the back from shoulder to waist. One thing was sure—with scars like that, Anamika would never participate in a beauty pageant again.

'I was also on duty many years ago when they brought Payal's body to the hospital. I had helped in the investigations and preparing the mortal remains for handing over to the family. The thing is, sahib, although it was a long time ago and I might be mistaken, the injury marks look the same.'

'I don't think you're mistaken,' said Renuka, fishing out her mobile to display the photo she had taken from the police report. They placed the two mobiles side by side, and the similarity was unmistakable. Four nearly parallel scratches, with a slight curve at the bottom, one of the marks slightly deeper and longer than the others.

'That's strange,' mused Rohit. 'If Payal was attacked by a leopard, as per the police report, how the hell did a leopard come into the garden to attack Anamika? That too in the middle of a party? It doesn't make sense. Two leopard attacks almost fifteen years apart.'

'What you say is true,' said Jagvati. 'There haven't been any reports of leopard attacks since that last one so many years ago. It's even more strange that a leopard should reappear like that,' she added, perplexed. 'It's almost as if it's the same leopard.'

'That's it,' said Rohit, jumping to his feet so fast that his chair toppled over with a clattering sound, which made everyone stop and stare in his direction. 'There's only one leopard that has been around for so long and that's our friend Tendu in the Mess. The leopard that I keep dreaming about.'

Renuka also got up excitedly and hugged him, 'I think you've solved the mystery. We must rush to the Mess.' Turning to the ayah, she gave her a hug too, 'Dadi, you've been a great help. Don't worry, we'll keep your secrets safe.'

'What about me?' asked Rehmat. 'Don't I get a hug too?' The two girls hugged each other in a tight embrace, Rohit placing his arms protectively around both of them. 'Take care, Rehmat,' he whispered. 'Stay at home till we solve this mystery.' As they exited, the buzz in the cafeteria returned to normal.

* * *

All those involved in the investigation were in the conference room office once again. Ravindran, Varinder,

Vikrant and the two young officers, Rohit and Renuka. They were mostly silent, waiting for the commandant to arrive. The atmosphere in the room was slightly oppressive, which the air conditioners did little to alleviate. There had been a massive thunderstorm the previous night, the rain coming down in big fat drops, heralding the arrival of the monsoons. The Ganga River had swollen and was a majestic sight, its waters stretching from bank to bank for more than a kilometre. The sandbanks that channeled the river during the dry months had all but disappeared, leaving only the occasional *char*, or river island, to break the flow of the river. Amidst the swirling waters were eddies and whirlpools with an undertow so strong that it could suck even an experienced swimmer under, only to deposit the lifeless body many miles downstream. Occasionally, a log could be seen floating down in deceptive serenity, for more often than not, it would be a crocodile preying on the unwary birds that flocked the riverbank.

The commandant entered and once seated, asked Varinder to commence the proceedings.

'As directed, Sir, the deputy had a long chat with Mukesh. Although not admitting it outright, he definitely knew Payal, but the extent of the relationship is as yet unclear. He has a history of violence, we are all aware of that, so he cannot be ruled out as a suspect.'

'I told him we suspect foul play in Payal's death, and it seemed to rattle him a bit,' added Ravindran. 'I asked him to sleep over it and to discuss it with his wife and then to meet me again today.'

'With due respect, Sir,' chimed in Vikrant, 'whatever his connection with Payal, I don't think he would ever harm Anamika or even allow her to be harmed. If anything, he's probably blaming himself for not being able to protect her. Looking out for her throughout the party, as we saw in the video, is not so much a sign of insecurity, it's more of protectiveness. And precisely in the half hour that he was sulking, she got attacked. He's blaming himself, that's the reason for his anger.'

'The youngsters have an interesting theory,' continued Varinder once Vikrant had stopped speaking. 'Perhaps we should hear them out.'

The commandant waved a hand in agreement in Rohit's direction. Renuka tapped him on the shoulder and gave him an encouraging smile. 'Go ahead, I'm sure we are right, even though it might seem silly.'

Rohit got to his feet and turned towards his audience. He told them briefly of all their findings, careful to keep Rehmat and the ayah out of the narration. 'When we saw the similarity of the injury marks, we thought of having a closer look at the leopard mounting in the Mess.'

'Surely you don't think our Tendu has suddenly come to life, do you?' said the commandant. 'That leopard has been dead for more than a century.'

'No, Sir, something like that, Sir,' fumbled Rohit. 'What I mean to say is that someone is masquerading or impersonating a leopard while carrying out these attacks. That's why the victims seemed so terrified. Yesterday, after coming to know of the similarities, we went to the Mess and had a closer look at the mounting. You've seen it a hundred times, the snarling face and outstretched paw ready to strike.'

'And what did you find? Did the paw give any clues?'

'Unfortunately Sir, the paw is very much attached to the rest of the body, We were so sure of ourselves that we got a bit stumped. We went around the mounting a few times and then noticed that the outstretched paw points directly to the tiger's claw displayed on the opposite wall. We opened this case and found tiny fibres embedded in the claws. It's almost as if the leopard was trying to redeem its honour after being unjustly maligned for so long. I'm no expert, Sir, but Renuka thinks it matches the dress worn by Anamika. Maybe forensics can confirm it.'

'We can get a forensics check done, Sir,' interrupted Renuka impatiently. 'But we women know and remember a dress and its colour forever and ever. I'm a hundred per cent sure the fabric stuck in the paw is the same, as are the claw marks.'

Everybody let out a nervous laugh, which broke the tension.

'I'm sure we cannot argue that point,' said the commandant. 'But tell me, what was I wearing?'

Renuka smiled at this obvious attempt to test her. 'Sir, we were all wearing our mess dress 6(B), don't you remember?'

The commandant smiled sheepishly but Renuka was in full flow. 'Mrs Menon was wearing a deep blue silk sari with a matching blouse, both with a golden *zari* border. Around her neck was a diamond necklace with matching studs and . . .'

'Stop, stop,' laughed the commandant. 'We believe you, don't we, boys?'

'That's all fine,' said the deputy, getting the meeting back on track. 'But where does it lead us to? Can we link Mukesh and the tiger claw in any manner?'

'Sir, he's also the Mess secretary and has the keys to the trophy cases. He was present when we were talking to the malis, leading to the disappearance of Dhani Ram and the murder of Mukhtiar. Plus his knowledge of the green rose. What more do we need?'

'It all still seems very circumstantial to me, but since he's coming to meet me in any case, I'll question him again.'

The commandant rose to go, 'Anything else?'

'Yes, Sir,' said Renuka and the commandant lowered himself with a martyred look, rolling his eyes in disbelief.

'You remember, Sir, last time I asked you about your neck, and you said it was fine; that you were just looking around for Jeevan? Well, Sir, I reviewed the footage and you're right, he's nowhere to be seen for most of the evening.'

'Nothing unusual about that,' said Vikrant. 'He has to supervise the other waiters and the layout of the dinner and keep things moving. He's not going to be hanging around. In any case, the photographer is there to take pics of the guests and not the staff. Let us not overanalyse everything.'

'Sorry, Sir, I just thought I should mention it,' said Renuka contritely.

'Anything else?' asked the commandant once again, pointedly. 'I hope we can go.'

'Actually, Sir,' began Rohit and the commandant groaned in disbelief, these youngsters were going too far. With a resigned look, he waited for Rohit to speak. 'I just wanted to know if we have got the call details from Mukhtiar's phone. If only we knew who he was in touch with that fateful night. That should clinch the case.'

Chapter 10

Curtain Call

Jeevan dressed himself carefully and looked at his image in the mirror. It was not his usual mess dress but a normal pajama-kurta similar to what the villagers wore. Unlike his crease-less and spotless mess dress, his clothes were stained and crumpled and gave off a rancid odour of sweat. He draped a worn and tattered cape around his shoulders. During the rains it served to keep out a light drizzle and also to conceal anything that one might be carrying. Leaving his lodge and carefully locking the door behind him, he skirted the Mess lawns and moved towards the gap in the wall, plucking a few of the green roses on his way out. Pausing a while to tuck in his pajamas and survey his surroundings, he went down the slope towards the mango orchard. No one saw him go and even if they did, what's one villager more or less? On reaching the orchard, he paced off a number of steps from one of the trees, the TREE as he was fond of calling it, ever since Mukhtiar had been found hanging from it. Having counted a hundred or so steps going deeper inside the grove, he stopped to brush away the undergrowth and reveal a small trapdoor. With the help of a rope, he lowered himself into the small room below, his hideout. On one side was a small shelf with an assortment of tools and what looked like gardening implements, shears and saws and such. On the other wall was a tunnel-like opening just wide and high enough to walk in a crouch. The end of the tunnel opened out at the river's edge, just a little above the high-water mark. An overhanging tree hid the entrance from outside. Inside the tunnel but tied to the tree was a small skiff which he pushed out and adjusted the rope that held it, till it floated on the river below. Satisfied with the arrangements, he pulled the boat back up. Of the many things that the army had taught him, and taught him well, was to always have a Plan B.

He retraced his steps to the hide-out, pulled himself up and went and sat down under his tree. He had sent Rehmat the note to meet in the rose garden and he knew Rehmat would come running, thinking it was from Rohit, the silly girl that she was, unnecessarily meddling in the affairs of grown-ups. Rohit and Renuka too, for that matter. Just because they were officers, they thought they could boss over him, a war veteran with the scars to show for it. Thinking about it caused his mind to wander, back in time to that fateful ambush. Bahadur had lived up to his name, not flinching in the furious enfilade that had come down on them. They had traversed that route many times, and on occasion even been part of the road-opening party that secured the route. Why that hillock was unoccupied that day remained unclear, the after-action report had glossed over the matter, without a care for the men who had died and got injured in the ambush. After the first fusillade, all those who could, had jumped out and returned fire, but in those crucial moments, it was only Bahadur who was standing by himself, firing from the hip. He could still vividly remember the moment Bahadur was hit, when perforce he had to stop to change magazines. Lying side by side in the drain by the side of the road, waiting for reinforcements to come, sporadically popping his head out to keep the terrorists at bay, he had seen his life ebb away, as Bahadur breathed his last. Just before that last shudder, Bahadur had gripped his collar saying, 'Look after Payal and my parents.'

He had in that moment sworn to himself that he would not allow anything to besmirch Bahadur's reputation.

Initially, he had consoled the parents and widow. He had even offered to marry Payal, but she had laughed in his face. Even that was fine, if in Bahadur's memory, she wanted to remain alone, the grieving widow, for a while. But then she started cavorting with Chaddha, a young officer. Chaddha should have known better, entertaining ladies in the Mess, spoiling both their reputations. So many people were commenting on her behaviour, behind Badlu Prasad's back, calling her the village whore. When he could stand it no longer, after she had spurned yet another proposal of marriage, he had followed Payal back one evening after she had left Chaddha's room. He had only intended to scare her with the tiger mask, but she had torn off his mask and seen his face, so he had no choice then but to finish her off. He had slashed at her with the tiger's paw that he had smuggled out of the display case, with a fury he did not know existed in him, oblivious to her terrified screams. He had no regrets though; Payal had got what she deserved. After all, the honour of the Regiment was paramount.

These girls these days just had no idea of what honour meant. How every action ultimately reflected on the Regiment. Anamika was no exception. Trying to seduce the young officers with her low-cut blouses and provocative moves. She had needed to be taught a lesson, just like Payal.

Just enough to make her behave. He had heard Mukesh and
Anamika arguing on a number of occasions, forgetting that
there were officers and ladies in the room, thinking they
were just wallflowers. He had only wanted to scratch her
face, enough to disfigure her so that nobody would look at
her again, no more beauty pageants. And also as an example
to the other ladies. But she had got startled and turned to
run, and he could only get one swipe in, down the length
of her back. At least he had scared her enough that she had
not appeared in public again. Mission accomplished.

But then Mukhtiar had to go and spoil it all. He had
enlisted his help to move the statues, rather than any of
the permanent Mess staff. That way no one would make
any connection. Who would have imagined that someone
would spot the changed position of the statues? Mukhtiar
had panicked when he heard that the entire working party
was to be questioned the next day. What should he do,
he had asked Jeevan over the phone? Maybe if he went
AWOL, absent without leave till the furore died down, it
would solve the problem? Realizing that Mukhtiar could
be a weak link, Jeevan offered to help, asking him to come
to the orchard after the 10 p.m. roll call, knowing that his
absence wouldn't be noticed till the 5 a.m. roll call the next
day. He made short work of drugging him and stringing

him up to make it look like suicide. It was just bad luck that the police investigated in more detail than was their wont. After all, they had hardly given Payal's case a second glance, conveniently declaring it a leopard attack. All because of that meddlesome duo of Rohit and Renuka.

Perhaps after dealing with Rehmat, he should take care of Renuka too? Just to teach her not to meddle in other people's affairs. Silly people, discussing everything while dining, while he stood within earshot in the doorway. And their 'operations room'? Absolutely laughable, leaving behind their notes and diagrams on the notice board for all to see. That's how he knew whom to target, what steps to take to throw them off his scent. Misplacing Bahadur's service record was enough to send them into a tizzy. In time they would learn of the changes he had surreptitiously made, with a little help from Jha, so that Badlu Prasad continued to draw a pension. That was his conscience at work. He had never sought any reward for himself, he had always served the Regiment loyally. And now Rehmat was following in Payal's footsteps, courting an officer, forgetting her station in life. Just another social climber, latching on to an officer fresh out of the Academy. He was certain her mother Zareena had planted this idea in her head, after seeing Rohit during the cocktails at the commandant's house. It would just not do for a third-generation officer to be romancing a village belle. It was his duty to make sure it didn't go any further, by taking care of Rehmat. He had the perfect plan in place, including leaving some green roses as clues, which would firmly point to Chaddha as the main suspect. That would serve him right, thought Jeevan, for stealing Payal away from him. With a contented sigh, Jeevan merged into the background to await Rehmat's arrival.

***

Priya Menon was having a cup of tea in the garden when Zareena came running up to her quite agitated, 'Madam, Rehmat hasn't come home from college yet. It's quite unlike her.'

Priya put her paper down and removed her reading glasses. 'Any idea where she could have gone? Maybe she has just gone out with her friends.'

Zareena hesitated a moment, 'Madam, of late she has been meeting Rohit baba often, sometimes alone and sometimes with Renuka.' Her voice trailing off, she asked, 'If you could please . . .'

'Of course,' said Priya, getting up and going inside. She called her husband on the landline. 'Hello? Yes, darling, I won't take much time. Zareena has just told me that her daughter Rehmat hasn't returned from college. Could you check with Rohit if he knows where she is? Yes, yes, I'll wait.' Turning to Zareena, she said, 'Rohit and Renuka are with the commandant only. He's just asking them. Hello? Yes, I see. Okay, just let me know.' She hung up and said, 'Zareena, Rohit has not seen her since yesterday afternoon when they met at the hospital. Rohit tried to call her, but she isn't picking up. But don't worry, my husband has asked the staff to look for her.'

'Thank you, Madam. Sometimes her phone is on silent, when she is attending classes. Still, I'm a little worried. Whenever she goes anywhere, she always tells me, that's how I know about her meetings with Rohit. So, it's strange. If you don't mind, Madam, may I go home? I can look around and ask people in the village too.'

Brigadier Menon put the phone down and turned towards the officers seated in front of him. 'I'm not happy with this latest development. My sixth sense tells me that something's not right.' He looked towards Rohit, 'I think the two of you should go around to the various places you've been meeting her.' Rohit opened his mouth to clarify but the commandant cut him off. 'Now is not the time. I'm not making any judgement. The first priority is to find Rehmat. She's as much my daughter as Zareena's,' he said, snapping his fingers towards the door. 'Off you go.'

'Ravindran,' he said once the two had left, 'call Mukesh and Anamika together for a chat. Invite them to your residence so that Mona is also around to smooth things over if things get awkward.'

'Yes, Sir,' said Ravindran and rose to go.

'Better still, Ravi, both of you go to their house instead. It'll give you a better feel of the situation, plus an opportunity to unofficially look around.'

'Good idea, Sir, I'll do just that.'

That left Varinder and Vikrant, the two staff officers with him. 'What's the latest on the mobile phone records?' he asked Vikrant. 'Any idea when we'll get the report?'

'It should have come in by now. If you'll permit me, Sir, I'll just go and check.' Waving him away, the commandant spoke to Varinder, 'I think you should get all the civilian staff together, especially the ones from this village. They can fan out and ask around. People are more likely to talk to them.'

Vikrant came in just then, face flushed with excitement. 'Sir, they've just managed to open the phone. There are no calls, only messages. The chats are between Mukhtiar and Jeevan, and it's Jeevan who called him to the orchard.'

'How do we know it's Jeevan?'

'The messages are from an unknown number, but Truecaller says it belongs to him.'

'Well, I'll be damned,' said the commandant. 'I wonder where he fits in. Better call him in for questioning.'

'You know, Sir,' said Varinder, 'I wonder whether it might not be better to go to his room and surprise him. Just like Chaddha, he also fits the bill on all counts, including, as Renuka pointed out, not being seen in the party videos.'

'Okay, let's do that. Vikrant, you stay here and hold the fort, while we go to the Mess. Just to be on the safe side, keep a quick reaction team on standby too.'

* * *

Rehmat was leaving the college talking excitedly with her friends when she saw Badlu Prasad waving at her from behind a line of cycle rickshaws. 'Namaste, Dadaji,' she greeted him. 'Do you have any more news for me?'

'No beta, nothing new. Just this,' and he handed over a piece of paper, which said, 'MEET ME ROSE GARDEN'. Rehmat was puzzled, the note was obviously from Rohit, but why had he not messaged? She rechecked her phone, but there was nothing there. In fact, Rohit had not seen any messages since a little before 8 a.m., which would have been just before their class hours. Probably that's why he sent me the note, thought Rehmat, as he wouldn't have been able to access his phone. She looked around, but Badlu Prasad had already shuffled off. She thought about leaving a message for her mother but she would be at work and in any case, the Mess and the commandant's house were adjacent to each other. After her meeting with Rohit, she would just hop across and they could come back home together.

With that settled, Rehmat started off towards the Mess, happy to be meeting Rohit, she hoped, by herself. The last couple of times, Renuka had always been around, the proverbial *kabab mein haddi*[4] and they hadn't been able to speak freely, let alone hold hands. Rohit would be leaving soon, and this could well be their last opportunity to spend some time together. They had so much to discuss and so little time. Lost in her thoughts, her feet automatically followed the path that led via the orchard to the gap in the Mess wall. Crossing the orchard, she looked up at the mango-laden trees. Thinking she would pluck a few mangoes on her way back, she hung her satchel containing her books and things on a protruding branch, so that she could slip through the Mess wall. Walking on, she saw an older man struggling to lift a sack of some sort. Coming nearer, she saw that it was none other than Jeevan. 'Jeevan *chacha*,' she said brightly, 'what are you doing here? May I help you?'

---

[4] A third wheel

'Oh *beta*, you are a godsend. I'm not as strong any more. I need to put this bag of manure in the shed over there.'

'I'll help you, chacha,' and they took one end of the bag each and shuffled deeper into the orchard. *What a gullible little fool she is*, thought Jeevan as they walked on; no one would be able to see them now. If anything, they would have seen a girl helping a man in village dress, nothing unusual or worth mentioning. They were huffing by the time they had covered fifty or so yards.

'Just a little bit further,' said Jeevan, setting the sack down and arching his back, as if in pain. Jeevan took out a water bottle, which he had laced with a sedative. 'Here, have some water.'

Rehmat drank gratefully from the proffered bottle, careful not to let it touch her lips. By the time they lifted the sack again, Rehmat was already wobbly on her feet and in less than a minute, slumped unconscious on the mouldy, leaf-strewn ground. Dragging Rehmat by her feet, he opened the trapdoor to his hideout and tying her hands and legs and taping her mouth, he shoved her unceremoniously inside. Taking out her mobile, he opened it, took out the battery and shoved it into his pocket. *Let her rot there*, he thought, looking down into the hideout, *nobody is ever going to find her*. And if they ever did, he would have an alibi.

Before closing the trapdoor, he tossed in a couple of the green roses he had plucked earlier, which would connect Chaddha to the crime scene. *Let's see how Chaddha wriggles out of this one.* Brushing off loose leaves and straightening his clothes, Jeevan left the orchard, looking around to ensure that he had left no tell-tale signs.

* * *

The commandant and Varinder were in the Officers' Mess. Inquiries revealed that Jeevan had not been seen since breakfast, nor was he in the office area. Rohit and Renuka had also reached the Mess while doing the rounds trying to find Rehmat. Rohit had tried to call her several times but kept getting a pre-recorded message. The four of them went down the path to the caretaker's lodge, which was tucked away on the slope leading to the river. Originally, it had been a guest house for visiting dignitaries, offering a splendid view of the river and bewitching sunsets. With the passage of time, it had gone into disrepair and now housed the Mess staff and surplus or discarded furniture.

'We need to get rid of all this junk,' said the commandant. 'Ask the deputy to speak to me. And this whole building could do with a face lift.' Varinder nodded and wrote in his notebook. Climbing the stairs to Jeevan's room, they found it locked. Varinder shook the shiny brass lock, giving it a few hard tugs, but it held firm.

'We'll have to break the lock, Sir, there's no other option.' Rohit went back down the stairs and after rummaging in the junk lying under the staircase, returned with an iron rod, with which he snapped open the lock.

The accommodation comprised two cosy rooms with a small kitchenette at one end. Bay windows overlooked a small, manicured lawn, no doubt the handiwork of the malis, with an uninterrupted view of the river beyond. The furnishings were spartan but well-maintained. Everything looked spick and span, as meticulously kept as the Mess he was responsible for. Where to look and what should they look for? At first glance, there was nothing to connect Jeevan with all the happenings.

'Let's each take one side of the room,' instructed the commandant. 'Don't touch anything unless absolutely necessary and replace everything exactly as you found it.'

Although the four of them rummaged through the room, they could not find anything of note. There was one photo of Jeevan and another jawan, both in uniform, alongside a pretty girl, who they surmised must be Bahadur and his wife Payal. Nothing suspicious about that. If only they could find the mobile Jeevan had used to communicate with Mukhtiar. Surely, he wouldn't be carrying that around.

'It's a long shot, Sir,' said Renuka, 'but why don't we try calling that number from Mukhtiar's phone? If it's on and somewhere nearby, we might be able to locate it.'

'Hmm, that just might work. Call the adjutant and ask him to make the call. Also ask him if there's any news of Rehmat's whereabouts.'

'I had given Rehmat a mobile to stay in touch with me,' said Rohit. 'I tried calling her, but there was no answer. Perhaps the adjutant can ask the police to check its location?'

Vikrant reported that he had called Jeevan's phone and that the number was ringing. The team in the room waited silently, straining to hear any sound. It was Renuka who held up a hand. 'I think I can hear some vibration from the direction of the balcony.'

They moved closer and soon heard a faint buzzing sound.

'I'll be damned,' said Varinder, looking at a decorative pile of stones in one corner, picking them up one by one. 'See, this one is a plastic moulded stone. We used to use these all the time to conceal cameras during operations.'

Turning the stone around, he slid open a panel to reveal the phone buzzing frantically inside. He cut the call and tried accessing the phone, but it was password-protected.

'That doesn't matter,' said the commandant, 'the connection between Mukhtiar and Jeevan is firmly established. Let's go catch the blighter.'

Varinder rang up the adjutant to tell him of their find. 'Send a lookout notice for Jeevan. Anyone seeing him anywhere should inform us, but on no account try to catch him or go anywhere near him.'

'Right, Sir,' replied Vikrant. 'On that other matter, Sir, Rehmat's phone is coming switched off, but her last known location was somewhere near the mango orchard.'

Rohit and Renuka looked worriedly at the commandant. 'Call two men from the residence guard and have them secure this room, just in case Jeevan returns. Also ask Vikrant to send the quick response team to the orchard. We will go there directly.'

They left the room and went back to the Mess building to where the cars were parked.

'Sir,' said Rohit. 'You go by car. Renuka and I will take the shortcut through the wall. That way we will be able to cover more ground.'

'Okay, do that. but watch your backs and keep your eyes peeled for Jeevan. I wonder where that blighter is.'

* * *

Jeevan was right there, hidden in plain sight. While returning to the Mess, he had seen the commandant's car speeding to the building. Scrambling through the gap in the Mess wall, he squatted amongst the bushes in the rose garden. In his village dress, he looked like one of the malis who worked in the Mess. Peeking through the bushes, he saw Rohit and Renuka join the commandant and Varinder as they went towards the lodge. He was not worried, there was nothing incriminating in his room. They would find nothing, as he was a master in the art of camouflage and concealment. His instructors had taught him well. 'Less is more' and 'hide in plain sight' were the most common phrases. Ironically, it was none other than Chaddha who had been his instructor during the field craft classes. Chaddha would be proud of him. How he, Jeevan, was within a few feet of him at the party, listening to every word of their argument. After the foursome had disappeared from view, he high-crawled to the ancient pipal tree that marked the boundary of the lawn. The tree had a small *machan* in its lower branches, often used to get a better view of the river, and he lithely climbed up and lay flat against the floorboards. From here he could see the lodge and the entire Mess premises. He would just wait here till everyone left, then return to the lodge, change into his working dress and take up his duties in the Mess. There was nothing to link him with anything. If and when an alarm was raised of Rehmat's disappearance, he might even join the search party and lead them on a wild goose chase. All in a day's work.

The sudden appearance of Renuka and Varinder on the balcony unnerved him, especially when Varinder started looking at the stones garden, picking up each one and turning them over. Varinder was the training officer after all, and such props were part of the training aids, used in teaching recruits. He saw the discovery of his hidden phone. Nothing wrong in that, many people kept more than one phone. As soon as the balcony was clear, he shimmied down and walked across casually to the cover of the bandstand. When the foursome passed by, he could hear fragments of their conversation. '. . . guards to secure the room . . .' and '. . . go to the mango orchard.' How had they homed in on the orchard so fast? And why were they securing his room? Was it only because it was unlocked now or was it something more? He saw the commandant and Varinder get into the car and leave, but then Rohit and Renuka came back and went towards the rose garden. There was definitely something afoot. Abandoning his plans to change, he decided to follow them, but first he had one more trick up his sleeve. Behind the bandstand were a number of old paint tins and an assortment of half-cut cans used for doing the whitewash. Selecting one of the cans, he retreated to the shelter of the pipal tree. Stripping down to his shorts he opened the can which contained a thick viscous paste the colour of brown mud, the colour of the statues. This paste had served him well earlier, and he proceeded to smear himself with it. Stuffing his clothes into a hollow of the pipal tree, he pulled from within it a ghillie suit which he slipped into. Smearing his hands and face once more with the camouflage paint, he proceeded towards the orchard. Within a few steps, he had merged wraith-like into the surroundings.

* * *

Rohit and Renuka reached the grove just as the quick response team (QRT) was pulling up. The dozen or so men that formed the QRT quickly dismounted and fanned out in a perimeter, as if reacting to some terrorist threat. Rohit called them and explained the situation to them.

'We are looking for a missing girl. We believe she might be somewhere here, it is the same place where Mukhtiar was found. We will carry out a sweep of the entire orchard and the forest beyond, right up to the river.' The jawans quickly spread themselves out and started walking carefully forward. Some of them were carrying lathis, which they used to sweep away the undergrowth or prod the ground. They had hardly walked a few dozen steps when there was a shout. 'Sahib, there's a bag here.' A quick look at the bag confirmed it was Rehmat's and reinforced their belief that she had to be somewhere close by. Rohit searched her bag carefully, trying to locate her mobile phone. He tried calling again but only received the standard pre-recorded message. Where could she possibly be?

* * *

Rehmat came to her senses with a throbbing pain in her leg. Straightening her leg, which was at an awkward angle under her, she groaned. She tried to piece together what had happened. She remembered helping Jeevan and drinking some water, but nothing after that. Had Jeevan drugged her and pushed her in here? Nothing made sense. Or was Jeevan the murderer after all? Who could have known that she would cross the grove to reach the rose garden? Had

Rohit indeed sent that note or was it a ruse to get at her? Were they even aware that she was missing? As her eyes adjusted to the light, she took stock of her situation. Using the wall as support, she managed to stand up with some difficulty. This made her feel dizzy again and she took a few moments to clear her head and look around. A little light filtered down through the trapdoor and it was enough for her to make out the outlines of the room. On one side, she could see a largeish opening from where a cool breeze was coming. On the other was a shelf with tools on it. The trapdoor was at least ten feet above her; there was no way she could reach it, even if her hands and feet had not been not bound. Maybe the shelf had something she could use to cut herself free or maybe if she toppled it over, she could stand on it and reach the trapdoor? Whatever she decided, it was up to her to get out of this predicament.

One thought kept troubling her, *Why me*? If at all Jeevan was to blame, what could he possibly have against her? She had heard the gossip in the village when they had seen her and Rohit together. Some of the villagers were affronted that she was seeing a boy, that too outside their *biradari*, their clan. Honour killings were not uncommon. Was this one of those things? Was Payal's death also an honour killing in the guise of a leopard attack? How on earth was there any honour in killing poor defenceless women? Her thoughts were interrupted by the sound of voices. Was she imagining it or had she heard Rohit's voice? She tried to listen more carefully.

'Sahib, there's a bag here,' she heard someone shout. Yes, they were looking for her and they had found her bag. Help was at hand.

She picked up some of the tools from the shelf with her bound hands, but none of them were sharp enough to cut through her bonds. She tried banging the tools against the shelf to make some noise, but with her hands tied behind her back, she could not get any leverage. Tears rolled down her cheeks, leaving mascara trails of frustration. The light filtering through the trapdoor was momentarily blocked out. Someone was right above her. *I'm saved*, she thought as she slumped to the floor.

* * *

The search party made steady progress through the orchard. It was generally open, though there were some patches with some undergrowth. The initial euphoria of finding Rehmat's bag was dying down. There were areas where one could see a fair distance ahead through the neatly laid out trees, but there was nothing much to see. Just as their spirits were beginning to flag, there was a shout from one side, 'Sahib, Sahib.' Asking the party to halt, Rohit and Renuka rushed in the direction of the call.

'Yes, what have you found?' Rohit asked the jawan on the far side of the search party.

'Nothing, Sir.'

'Then why did you call out?' asked Rohit.

'I never called out, Sir. In fact, the shout had come from that direction,' replied the jawan, pointing further towards the river.

'Maybe someone has gone ahead on his own,' suggested Renuka, but a headcount revealed that all were present. Puzzled, Rohit ordered the search to recommence, reporting back to the commandant of the progress. The commandant asked Rohit to stop the column and to return to the positions they were at when the call was heard.

Walking into the orchard, the commandant looked around. Everything looked absolutely as it should be, it was nature at its best. The neatly laid out rows of trees laden with fruit, the mulchy ground beneath their feet, deadening their footfalls.

'Have you seen the lapwings in the garden?' asked the commandant.

'Of course, Sir,' replied Rohit, a little puzzled. 'As a child, I would often chase them around.'

'And?'

Rohit thought for a moment and then it dawned on him why the commandant was asking this question. 'They lay their eggs on the ground and should anyone come close by, they purposely draw you in the wrong direction.'

'*Shabash*, Rohit,' exclaimed the commandant, slapping him on the back. 'So let's concentrate on where we are now: My sixth sense tells me we're close. Tell everyone to grab a stick and move slowly ahead, prodding the ground continuously as if clearing a minefield.'

* * *

Jeevan lay prone on the ground watching the movements of the search party. How had they come here so soon? He had drugged Rehmat only enough to knock her out temporarily, so that he would have an alibi for later. If she were to regain consciousness, she would be able to identify him. He didn't want to, but now he would have to silence her for good before she was found. He had to find a way to divert the search party's attention long enough for him to reach the trapdoor unobserved. Then he could drag Rehmat down the tunnel shaft, blocking it behind him and making good his escape. He would untie her and push her into the river where she would be swept away.

Using the boat, he could then drift a little downstream and join the search party as if nothing had happened. He could still get away with it. Even if they uncovered the pit, they would find it empty, except for the green roses, and if at all they found the tunnel shaft, he would have been long gone. Now all he had to do was to distract them. His earlier attempt had not succeeded; the commandant had seen through that subterfuge. Now he would have to make a stronger demonstration. Inching back until he reached a depression in the ground, he removed the ghillie suit. It had served its purpose, and would come in handy once more. Selecting a nearby tree, he climbed up a little way and suspended the suit so that it looked like a hanging body. After Mukhtiar's discovery, they would definitely be sensitive to another hanging. Now, how could he attract their attention? From his pocket, he removed Rehmat's phone and re-inserted the battery. Switching it on, he saw that there were numerous missed calls and messages, mostly from Zareena and Rohit. Jeevan was certain that they would call again. Adjusting the volume to high, he placed it inside the suit and expertly melted away into the shadows.

As anticipated, the phone rang, its shrill tones startling everyone concentrating on the search.

'It's Rehmat's phone,' screamed Renuka, holding her own phone aloft, and running in the direction of the sound. Seeing her, Rohit and the others started running too, the search party breaking its orderly line. This was just the opportunity Jeevan was waiting for. Loping across the wooded area, he quickly eased open the trapdoor and slithered inside. The opening would not be as well camouflaged as before, but hopefully the false grass and leaves pasted to the top would pass a cursory glance. Just as he closed the trapdoor, he heard some shouts. They must have found the suit.

* * *

Rohit came to an abrupt halt when he saw the ghillie suit dangling from the tree. His blood ran cold, and he had a sudden cramp in his stomach, which doubled him over. 'No, no, no,' he screamed, louder and louder, not daring to look up. One of the jawans hoisted his buddy on his shoulders, who reached up and yanked at the suit. 'This is just an empty suit,' he said, much to everybody's consternation and relief. Rohit looked up and breathed again. Renuka held him across the shoulders, comforting him.

'It's all right, Rohit. We'll find her. Don't lose heart.'

'Okay everyone,' he ordered, standing tall once more, 'back to where we were. Let's keep searching.'

He looked up to see the commandant watching him, flapping his arms, as if imitating a bird and turning back to the direction from they had come. *Darn it*, thought Rohit, *the lapwing trick has fooled us not once but twice.*

Rehmat was backed up against the wall when someone dropped inside. When the trapdoor had opened briefly, she thought her ordeal was over. Then the door closed, and it was dark again. She had just enough time to make out that someone dark-skinned and bare-bodied, had slithered backwards into the hideout. Was it Jeevan again? She struggled against her bonds, trying to scream, but to no avail. She sensed, rather than heard, some movement of a heavy object. Suddenly, she was yanked forward, falling to the ground with a thud, wincing in pain when her body hit the ground. She felt a slight breeze blowing in her face and she realized she must be facing the entrance to some passageway. A foot prodded her forward.

'Get in there,' she heard Jeevan say. 'Just do as I say, and I won't hurt you.'

Nothing doing, thought Rehmat, *I'm not going into that passage.* From her prone position, she kicked backwards with all her might, catching Jeevan squarely in the chest, sending him crashing into the shelf, with a clatter of falling tools.

'Did anyone hear that?' asked Rohit raising his hand to signal everyone to halt.

'Yes, Sir,' said several voices in unison.

'I think it was from somewhere underneath there. Look sharp, boys, look for some opening in the ground.'

'Here, Sir,' said a jawan, kneeling on the ground with a hand raised. Rohit hurried to the spot and knelt beside him, brushing away a few loose twigs. There was no doubt about it, it was a trapdoor, cleverly coated with false grass. Grasping it with both hands, he heaved it open. Looking down, he could see the fallen shelf and pinned beneath it, Rehmat, her legs flailing in despair. *At least she's alive*, he thought as he lowered himself carefully into the hole, making sure not to step on anything that would put more pressure on Rehmat's prone body. He shoved the shelf aside and pulled Rehmat upright, and put his arms around her.

'You're safe now,' he whispered, wiping away her tears. 'I'll always be there for you.'

Epilogue

When Jeevan saw Rohit peering down into the hideout, he knew the game was up. He gave the shelf a mighty heave, trapping Rehmat under it. Pulling her out would give him just enough time to make good his escape. Slithering backwards into the tunnel entrance, he thought of blocking it by collapsing the roof of the tunnel but gave up when he saw Rohit jumping down. The light was fading, and he made his way down the tunnel carefully, his eyes soon adjusting to the dark. Behind him, he could hear confused shouting as instructions were passed to pull Rehmat out.

He stopped for a while to catch his breath. There was silence all around. Had they forgotten about him? His relief was short-lived as he heard the sounds of people clambering down, and the exultant shout when the tunnel entrance was discovered. He had no time to lose, he could already see the beams of flashlights darting into the tunnel.

Ignoring his pursuers, Jeevan quickly covered the rest of the distance to the opening overlooking the river. He sighed in relief when he saw his boat and cautiously eased it down to the water, where it bobbed up and down. He tested the rope and carefully slid down into the boat, just as a jawan showed up at the opening, shouting for him to stop and pulling at the rope that still bound the boat to the tree on the riverbank. Sitting down in the boat, he pulled out a small oar, and with a mock salute, set the boat free.

Freed from its tether, the boat lurched and was soon swept away by the current. By now, some of the jawans had reached the riverbank after running through the orchard. They could clearly see Jeevan waving at them, one hand steering the boat with the oar, taking it further midstream, trying to reach the other bank. They could only watch in horror when the small boat caught the swell of one of the whirlpools. Jeevan flailed the oar this way and that but could not break through. The small boat went round once, then twice, before being sucked into the current, the oar bobbing up once, before it too disappeared from view. The police were notified and both the banks of the river were searched for up to 20 km downstream. A few sightings were investigated, but they turned out to be false alarms. After a few days, the police closed the case, declaring it an accidental death.

It was time to bid au revoir to Fatehpuri. The young officers were packed and ready to go, their shiny black trunks lined up waiting for the transport to take them to the railway station. As a special gesture, the commandant and his wife had come to see them off. Zareena and Rehmat were also there, standing a little to the back. The officers got into the waiting vehicles, which moved off one by one. Rohit signalled for the others to go ahead; he would come in the last car. When only he remained, Rehmat came forward to stand beside him. They held hands silently, not knowing what to say. The last few days had been so tumultuous and if anything, had brought them even closer together. The clock was ticking; he would have to leave soon if he was to be on time to catch the train. He remembered how he used to feel when his father had to depart after his spells of leave. Somehow, the parting always seemed harder for those who stayed back. Neither of them wanted to make the first move. It was the commandant who broke the stalemate.

'For heaven's sake, man, just give her a ruddy kiss!,' on hearing which, Rehmat shyly hid her face in her hands and darted off, pigtail bouncing joyously and alluringly from side to side.

Scan QR code to access the
Penguin Random House India website